How to Write an Emotionally Resonant Werewolf Novel

Stories by Alex Miller

How to Write an Emotionally Resonant Werewolf Novel

Stories by Alex Miller

Acknowledgements

Some of the stories in this collection originally appeared in the following publications: *Barely South Review*, "Music Row" (published as "This is Nashville); *Bartleby Snopes*, "Emoland;" *The Binnacle*, "Smoking and Other Bad Decisions;" *Black Wire Literary Magazine*, "Thermite" and "Mandy;" *The Boiler Journal*, "The Layoff;" *The Bombay Literary Magazine*, "This Place Can Be Beautiful Again;" *Contraposition*, "Death Cult;" *The Dead Mule School of Southern Literature*, "Mule Day;" *Dr. Hurley's Snake Oil Cure*, "Skipping School," *Fifth Wednesday Journal*, "Jamie;" *Galavant*, "Gestation Crate;" *Maudlin House*, "How to Write an Emotionally Resonant Werewolf Novel;" *New Wave Vomit*, "From a Safe Distance" and "Love in the Time of the Etruscans" (published as "2 a.m."); *The Ofi Press*, "The Loneliness of the Retail Banker" (published as "Infidelity"); *One Title*, "You Are Not Eighteen Anymore;" *Open Road Review*, "Today We Are Still Married;" *Queen Vic Knives*, "Who Are You? I'm a Bear;" *Rabbit Catastrophe Review*, "An Invisible Place above Us;" *The Sandy River Review*, "Kandahar;" *Screaming Seahorse*, "The Worst Chinese Restaurant in Detroit;" *We Feel Pretty*, "Michelle and Rockets;" *WhiskeyPaper*, "Fawn;" *Thunderclap*, "You Can Have It All"

TABLE OF CONTENTS

For Shelly. Who came to the party.

Gestation Crate

I'm one of those girls who used to go crazy over unicorns. When I was a kid, I had all the plastic toys and stuffed animals and a big color poster on the wall behind my bed. And I'd look up at it at night when I should have been asleep, and I'd think about how great it would be to ride a unicorn, hold on to its snow-white mane as it galloped through an enchanted forest, charge into battle against grimlocks and blood sorcerers. Some nights I'd look out my bedroom window at the lawn all lit up from the lights of the house. I always hoped to see a unicorn. I kept hoping and hoping, until one day I was too old for unicorns.

They say the reason girls get obsessed with horses is because they want sex. Only maybe their psyches aren't yet developed to where they can really understand sex, so instead they imagine straddling some big strapping Clydesdale and letting it bounce them up and down. They say it's all psychological. I don't know much about that, but I do know I started feeling sexual at a young age. I guess I was eight or nine. Maybe that's young and maybe it's not. I remember how my brother—he was about five years older than me—used to have his friends over sometimes to watch sports on the big TV in the basement. My brother wasn't real keen on hanging out with his kid sister, but if I kept quiet and stayed in the back of the room, he'd let me stick around. And I wouldn't have bothered him at all if it hadn't been for his friend, Jack. I didn't give a shit about most of my brother's friends, but there was something different about Jack. I don't know. He barely even talked to me. I just liked to look at him, is all. I'd hang out in the back of the basement while Jack and my brother watched basketball on TV. And I'd lie on a couch with a blanket over me. And

I'd put a basketball between my legs, and then I'd just stare at Jack and quietly go to town on the basketball.

Something about Jack made me feel very sexual. I didn't know exactly what sex was, but I'd watched enough TV to know there was something men and women did naked under the covers. And Jack made me feel something else, too. Something beyond sexual. When I looked at him, I felt like I was far up in the sky, like I could float around and didn't have to worry about falling, and I could see the whole world below me, with green hills and blue streams winding between them, and if I wanted, I could go anywhere, to Paris or Egypt or Australia. When I looked at Jack, I felt like the life I was living was one of limitless possibilities.

I always hoped something real would happen between me and Jack, but he was in high school and too old for somebody's kid sister. I kept hoping he'd ask me to be his girlfriend. I kept hoping and hoping until one day I understood.

* * *

When I consider how much I used to think about sex, it seems funny how long it took me to get knocked up. I was always pretty crazy about birth control. That's what saved me for so long. But I wasn't crazy enough, I guess, in the end. My boyfriend Riley was not exactly thrilled to hear about it, but he acted decent, after a while, after it sunk in. He thought it was important we keep it. I didn't care much either way, but Riley felt strongly about it. I'd never seen him get so worked up about anything. He promised to work harder to find a job. And he said it earnestly, while holding my hand and looking into my eyes. This sort of behavior was unusual. What can I say about Riley? He was no Jack. He sure as Christ was no unicorn.

I remember waking up one morning right after I started to show. The alarm went off, playing some Taylor Swift love song, and I slapped the button to shut it up. Riley lay beside me. He snored and rolled over. I brushed my stomach with the tips of my fingers. I imagined the thing inside me, sucking away, leeching nutrients from my blood.

I got up and went to the kitchen. I checked my email on a laptop on the table. I hoped to hear back about a job I'd applied for. I'd applied two weeks earlier but hadn't heard a thing. Some magazine wanted an editorial assistant. It wasn't a magazine I cared anything about, but it was a real job, the kind I'd never had. And I was qualified, with a journalism degree and everything. I'd gone to college and the whole time planned on living a real life. Somehow it hadn't worked out for me. I never landed a serious job, never even found an internship. Eventually I gave up and took a shit job at the mall. I figured I'd just keep working the shit job till I died.

In my email, I had a message from an animal welfare group. The group was upset over something called gestation crates. A video was embedded in the email. The video contained footage shot surreptitiously at a pig warehouse. The video showed pigs in small cages. The bars of the cages were covered in rust or shit. The pigs squealed. The pigs banged their heads against the bars, but there was no room for the pigs to move. Shit pooled on the concrete floor. The pigs lay in pools of their own shit. When the camera panned around, you could see that the rows of pig cages stretched on and on, pretty much forever. The warehouse looked like hell, some kind of pig hell. The pigs had purple sores on their hides. The pigs stood up and stamped their feet. The pigs slipped and fell into pools of their own shit. The pigs squealed and squealed.

"The fuck are you watching?" Riley said.

He came out of the bedroom and sank into the couch. He turned on the TV and PS3. He held a controller and played Killzone.

"I'm watching bacon," I said. "Are you looking for a job today?"

"I'll get to it," he said. He pressed buttons on the controller. He launched a rocket at a tank.

"It would be a big help if you found a job," I said.

"I'll get to it," he said. He pushed more buttons. He shot an alien in the face.

I went to work. I spent a long time folding shirts. Folding shirts was an important part of my job. I folded shirts before we opened in the morning, and all day long customers came into the store and unfolded them. When they left, I folded the shirts again.

I arranged some pastel hoodies for a new display in front of the store. A song by Michael Bublé played over the speakers. I thought it was unfair to make my fetus listen to Michael Bublé. Listening to Michael Bublé would make my unborn child demented, or make it so when she came out, she'd only have three fingers and a stunted leg.

One of the shirts had a unicorn on it. I looked at the unicorn. I thought about the poster that had hung in my bedroom when I was a kid. I'd been a happy kid, the kind who always had a lot of dreams. A shit job at the mall was not among them. Neither were babies.

"Stop daydreaming," Tyler said. Tyler was my boss. Tyler was assistant manager.

"Sorry," I said.

I tried to fold shirts faster. Tyler didn't walk away. He looked at me and smirked. He looked like he was imagining having sex with me, and not in a nice way. Tyler looked like all his sexual fantasies were porno fantasies.

Later two girls came into the store. They were about sixteen and blond and wore jean shorts almost too small to be shorts. They talked about Katy Perry and bounced a little as they walked.

"Can I help you find anything?" I said.

But the girls didn't answer. They walked by me and kept talking about Katy Perry. They went to a rack of clothing and looked through it. One of them held up a blouse, and the other laughed.

"I'd rather shoot myself in the face," said the girl holding the blouse.

I stood in the middle of the sales floor and watched them. It didn't matter because they didn't see me. I was invisible. And it hadn't been so many years since I was a girl just like them. The kind of girl who boys whisper about in study hall. The kind who can eat anything and not worry because she's never been fat, never even imagined being fat. With one hand I rubbed my stomach, rubbed the bulge. Most of it was the baby. But I knew if I tried squeezing into a pair of shorts like those girls wore, the fat in my legs would ooze out like the Blob, and everybody would take a good look at my cellulite and weird veins. I stood on the sales floor and imagined how I'd look, and it was awful. Somebody would call the police.

Tyler walked up and stood beside me. He looked at the girls like he wanted to have sex with them, and not in a nice way.

"We need to get some girls like those to work here," he said. "Girls like those would bring men into the store."

Traffic on the way home was bumper to bumper. I punched buttons on the radio but didn't find any songs I liked. The car suddenly seemed small. It was a regular-sized car, but suddenly it felt so small I could hardly breathe. I imagined having a wreck and being trapped in the car, imagined the steel frame pinning me to my seat. I would try to slide out a window, but I wouldn't be able to move because the engine block would have crushed the bones in my legs. Metal would be everywhere. I would feel it pierce my belly. I would feel it pressed against my face.

* * *

At home, Riley lay on the couch playing Killzone.

"Did you look for a job today?" I said.

"I'm fighting the last boss," Riley said.

The last boss was a skull guy with armor. The last boss teleported around. Riley tried to shoot him, but he teleported and killed Riley's character. This happened a few times.

"Fuck," Riley said. "Goddamn fuck."

He held up the controller like he would throw it into the TV. Then he sank back into the couch. He pressed a button and started fighting the boss again.

I sat at the kitchen table and opened my laptop. I smelled something awful from the kitchen. The dishes hadn't been washed. Somehow the dishes never got washed.

I checked my email. I wanted an email from the magazine but didn't get one. I wondered how long I would go on hoping. Because it wasn't like the magazine would tell me if they didn't want me. They just wouldn't say anything. It's easier to say nothing. And I would keep on like this for a few more weeks, feeling that hopeful, fluttery feeling in my chest whenever I opened my email. Eventually I would take the hint. And I wouldn't feel too let down, because this is always how it's been for me. My life isn't the kind where good things just suddenly happen, like lightning out of a clear summer sky. Things would go on like they always had. I'd keep working at the boutique until I was too old and ugly, then I'd move across the mall to some sad store for old, ugly women.

I saw the email from the animal welfare group again. I opened it and watched the gestation crate video. I watched pigs flop around in their shit. Some of them had bloody wounds on their legs. One of them had a bone sticking out of her knee. She flopped around and got shit all over the wound. I smelled the stink of unwashed dishes. The pigs squealed in their cages. They pressed their faces against the bars. The pigs squealed and squealed.

Without even thinking, I rubbed my stomach. I looked at the walls of the apartment. They were covered in yellow wallpaper with some faded filigree design. The apartment was very old. There were food stains all over the wallpaper, tiny oblong spots of red and brown. I rubbed my belly and wondered why anyone bothered having babies. What was the point if the world was full of ugly wallpaper and shitty jobs at the mall and traffic jams and kitchen sinks full of scummy dishes and putrescence?

That's what I thought about all night. I went to sleep thinking about it, and thought about it again when I woke up around 2 a.m. I didn't say a word on the way out. I took the stairs down and went outside to where I'd parked the car down the street. I sat in the car for a while before starting the engine. I just listened to myself breathe, in and out. I touched my stomach. I drove slow at first and took the car to the highway. I remember how my headlights lit up the road and how empty it looked, as if someone had built it just for me. I looked at the highway as it stretched long into the distance, stretched farther than I could know. I thought maybe I'd just floor it for a few hours and see where that got me. Then I'd pull over and get something to eat, and maybe I'd find a store selling little knick-knacks and shit, and maybe I'd buy one of those pewter unicorn figurines like I had when I was a kid, and I'd hang it from the rearview mirror. Then I'd get back on the highway and drive some more.

FROM A SAFE DISTANCE

One night the girl who works at the desk across from mine said "fuck" when her computer crashed, and I turned and saw both her middle fingers raised as she growled—a little—instead of crying, her body twisting at the waist, hair falling across her eyes, head tilted so I could see the flow of her jaw, and I thought about saying something nice, like "actually you are beautiful"—except I'd never risk anything so corny—so I thought if she asked—and it's not like we ever talk so it was a safe bet she'd never ask—I'd tell her it was like watching a tsunami or an erupting volcano, only I'm standing on a hilltop with birds, and I'm far enough away but can still feel the ground shake, can hear all of nature roaring my name.

EMOLAND

I've known a lot of morons in my life and met most of them at school. Here in Emoland I go to school five days a week. Sometimes I think Emoland would be better without school. I think it quite a lot, actually.

I've always taken the bus to school, and I noticed when Alyssa started riding again. Troy used to drive her in his Chevy, but after he dumped her she came back to the bus. Alyssa wasn't my friend, but sometimes she sat with me because I was the only other high school person on the bus. We were just freshmen, but technically that counts as high school. All the little kids acted scared of us. In Emoland, big kids could be very dangerous. Alyssa almost never talked to me. I wanted to ask her all about Troy, about what it was like to date a big shot from the wrestling team. Time and again, I chickened out. Alyssa was extremely hot.

It felt weird to sit beside someone and not say anything. It felt like I wasn't really there at all, like I watched from a distance, like in a dream. It wasn't the first time I'd felt that way. Lately I'd felt that way quite a lot.

* * *

Charles was the best teacher in Emoland. He taught English. The best teachers are always English teachers. Charles wanted us to call him Chuck. The thing about Charles was he tried so hard to act like one of us kids, and it was sad because he came off like some pathetic old guy who couldn't cope. I refused to call him Chuck. I called him Dr. Weirdbeard.

On the first day of school, Dr. Weirdbeard told us his class would be different. He showed us a big copy of *David Copperfield* by Charles Dickens.

"I promise I will never make you read Charles Dickens," he said. "If I made you read Dickens, you'd hate me and hate English class and never read anything again except *Twilight*, which doesn't even count."

Then he started ripping pages out of *David Copperfield*.

"Screw Dickens," he said.

Torn pages fluttered through the air and settled on the floor in front of his desk.

"Screw Dickens," he said.

That was a few months ago. More recently he's had us read *The Loneliness of the Long Distance Runner*. It's OK.

One day in class, Troy wouldn't leave Avery alone. Nobody ever left Avery alone, so Troy probably thought Avery was an easy target. Troy was right.

Troy asked Avery—really loud so everybody could hear—where he bought his blue jeans. At first Avery wouldn't answer, but Troy kept asking him louder and louder. Finally, Avery said in a small voice that his mom bought them at Walmart. Troy laughed and laughed.

The thing about Troy was that he lived in his own little world. In Troy's world, there were only two kinds of people—cool people and nerds. In Troy's world, nerds deserved to be punished by the cool people. Troy's world had no more depth than this.

Troy considered himself a cool person because he played sports. It didn't matter to him that nobody liked him, not even the other athletes. In Troy's world, being good at sports and winning medals is what makes you cool. Troy played pretty much every sport, but wrestling was the one he liked to brag about. He had a natural gift for crushing people and holding them down.

Anyway, it made me angry how he laughed at Avery, so from my desk across the aisle I called Troy a nematode.

"What the fuck are you even talking about?" Troy said.

"You're what I'm fucking talking about. You're a dumb nematode. You're so dumb, you don't even know what a nematode is."

"Sure I do," he said.

"What's a nematode?"

"Shut up," Troy said.

Troy was very pissed.

After class, Dr. Weirdbeard pulled me aside and told me he liked how I "handled myself back there." He asked me some lame questions like if I enjoyed being in high school and what I did for fun. I probably should have lied and told him I spent all my free time reading the classics of Western literature, but instead I told him the truth, which is that I played a video game called *World of Orcs*. It's one of those big games that everybody plays online, and it's like a whole other world where people level up and fight orcs. Dr. Weirdbeard told me it sounded "rad" and he'd like to play it sometime. I gave him my server ID so he could find me in the game.

Alyssa sat with me again on the bus-ride home. I worked up the nerve to ask her about Troy.

"We're not really broken up," she said. "Not really. This is just temporary."

"Everybody says he dumped you," I said.

"He'll change his mind. Guys always do," she said. "He loves me. He just doesn't know it right now."

"Why would you want to get back with some jerk who dumped you?"

"I love him," she said. "You wouldn't understand, not unless you've loved someone. He'll take me back someday because I love him so much."

I told Alyssa about *World of Orcs*. I told her Dr. Weirdbeard was going to play with me.

"That's creepy," she said. "That kind of thing ends up on the six o'clock news."

I asked her to play with us, and she told me she'd think about it. That's how the three of us started playing *World of Orcs* together. Stranger things have happened in Emoland, but not many.

* * *

Dr. Weirdbeard chose a character that was like an archer who could speak to animals. Alyssa made a dark knight with a big sword and some kind of tight leather bathing suit for armor. I played a druid because I liked casting spells to heal people.

Dr. Weirdbeard and Alyssa helped me with my quest to kill the Orc Lord. He's a giant orc who wields a mighty scimitar. He's mean to the other orcs and makes them do bad things. That's why I had to kill him. Also, I wanted his mighty scimitar.

Dr. Weirdbeard started shooting arrows at the Orc Lord, and Alyssa stepped up to fight him face to face, and I cast heal spells on everybody. It had all the ingredients of a fool-proof plan except that it failed pathetically. The Orc Lord killed Alyssa with one chop of his mighty scimitar. Then he killed me. Then Dr. Weirdbeard ran away.

"Dying sucks," Dr. Weirdbeard said.

"I know," I said.

Then I typed "/dance" and my druid started dancing. Pretty soon all of us danced together.

"I don't know how to dance in real life," I said.

"It helps if you don't think about it," Dr. Weirdbeard said. "It helps if you're drunk."

I typed "LOL."

"Forget I said that," he said.

"No, it's true," Alyssa said. "Dancing is easiest when you're drunk."

"I'm going to lose my job," Dr. Weirdbeard said.

* * *

The next day in school, Dr. Weirdbeard's eyes looked red and dry, and he hadn't finished grading our quizzes. He told me he'd been awake all night "grinding up levels." He gave me a grin and a wink, but after that he switched into teacher mode, and he stood in front of the class for an hour talking about Alan Sillitoe and working-class fiction and the importance of rebelling against the class system in late 1950s England, and it was difficult to reconcile this boring teacher-figure with the friend who I'd stayed up late with playing video games.

A few hours later I saw him again, sort of by accident. I was walking to algebra, my last class of the day, and I caught a glimpse of Dr. Weirdbeard when I passed by the open door of the teachers' lounge. I stopped and stared for a minute. He drank coffee with the other teachers, all old women with bad hair. One of them complained about her "little monsters in third period." All the old women laughed, but Dr. Weirdbeard looked down at his coffee cup and rubbed his temples. Dr. Weirdbeard looked like he wanted to shoot himself in the face.

On the bus home, Alyssa didn't talk about Troy. She talked about *World of Orcs*.

"We can totally beat the Orc Lord," she said.

"Totally," I said. "Use your Hell Slash attack. It focuses all your rage and hate into your sword. Just keep spamming Hell Slash until he dies."

That night, the three of us played World of Orcs again. When we found the Orc Lord, Alyssa did just as I told her. She hit him in the face with Hell Slash. But then he sliced her with his mighty scimitar, and she almost died. I saved her with a heal spell. She hit him over and over with Hell Slash, and I kept healing her, and Dr. Weirdbeard ran around in circles pelting the Orc Lord with arrows. Pretty soon we'd won.

"This is so rad," Dr. Weirdbeard said.

I looted the mighty scimitar, but instead of keeping it, I gave it to Alyssa. It glowed purple when she equipped it. She took a few practice swings, wielding it like she was a sexy demon from my nightmares.

* * *

Late at night after we'd logged off, I was trying to fall asleep when my cell phone lit up from a text. It was Alyssa. She wanted to go somewhere. I texted back that I'd go anywhere. A half-hour later I sneaked out of the house, and she picked me up at the end of my driveway in her father's minivan. This was risky because she was too young to drive. When I brought up this point, she told me to stop acting like a pussy.

Alyssa drove us to the school, to the football field. Our school had a very large stadium. Football is quite popular in Emoland. The lights were out, so everything looked dark. We walked on tiny blades of manicured grass. Being out there at night, somewhere I wasn't supposed to be, it made me feel—I don't know—I guess it made me feel like a ghost.

"This is where Troy fucked me for the first time," Alyssa said as we approached the fifty-yard line. "After the homecoming game last year, after he scored the winning touchdown. After the dance he took me out here, just the two of us, and it was nice."

"What's it like to have sex?"

"We almost didn't," she said. "He couldn't get it up. We had to fool around for an hour, and then when we got to it, it didn't last long. It was nice though, to be naked on the grass under the stars."

"You talk about him a lot."

"He's all I think about."

"Think about something else. Something better."

"Make me forget him," she said. "I don't ever want to think about him again."

So I kissed her. This was the first time I'd ever kissed a girl in Emoland, and her lips were soft and wet, and her face felt warm. I held her head as I kissed her and ran my fingers through her hair. We knelt and made out some more, and I pawed her breasts from outside her shirt, and she grabbed at my crotch, but we didn't take off our clothes or do anything that could get her pregnant. I hoped she wouldn't think I was a pussy. I felt like I'd be ready soon but not that night. Sex was a big deal to me because it only happens in the real world. Once you have it, you can't ever go back to Emoland.

After we finished, Alyssa looked at the sky. The wind cut sharp and cold against my face, and I watched it blow waves through her hair.

"I like it outside," she said. "I feel free. I feel—I don't know— the way birds must feel, like I can go anywhere."

I leaned back in the grass and watched her some more. The moonlight painted her blue. That's how I like to remember her, blue and ecstatic and looking to the stars.

✳ ✳ ✳

It didn't take long for word to get around school that we'd fooled around. In Emoland, everybody is always in everybody else's business. The next day I heard people whispering about me in the hallways. Upperclassmen I'd never met before high-fived me. But then Troy showed up, and things happened fast. He shoved me from behind. I dropped my books, saw them scatter across the floor. A crowd moved in to witness my humiliation.

"Listen up, nerd," Troy said, putting his finger in my face and spitting a little. "From now on, you keep your nerdy hands off my girl."

"She's not your girl," I said.

"She's my girl if I say she's my girl."

"Your girl says you can't get it up. Your girl says you can't even last five minutes."

Everybody laughed. Troy stomped away. And as I picked my books off the floor, it occurred to me that happy endings were possible, even in Emoland.

Later in English class, Dr. Weirdbeard's eyes were red again, and he kept putting his head down on the desk. He'd graded our quizzes at last. He called me to his desk to give me mine and explain that while he enjoyed *World of Orcs*, it had intruded on his real life. He told me he couldn't play anymore.

"At some point," he said, "everybody must accept reality. Even me. Even when reality isn't what we want it to be."

I told him I understood. I told him it was probably for the best. But secretly I felt bummed. It's nice to have a friend to play games with, even if he's your teacher and somewhat embarrassing, even if he's not very good at the game, even if he always tries to speak to the animals when he should be shooting them with arrows for experience points.

At the end of the school day, Alyssa didn't take the bus. She didn't log in to *World of Orcs* that afternoon, either. I played by myself for an hour and killed some boars. Later I went outside on the deck in the back of my mom's house. I looked at the hills in the distance, and they were full of trees. Afternoon gave way to evening, and as the sun set it painted colors on the clouds. Sometimes the real world can be a very beautiful place.

* * *

The majesty of nature is a wonderful thing, but it can also be quite boring. After I got tired of staring at the trees and the sky and everything, I logged back into the game. I helped some random girl kill twenty manticores for a quest. She told me her name was Sancha and she lived in Holland. I asked her all about Holland, and she asked me about the U.S.

"I don't know the first thing about America," I said. "But I can tell you all about Emoland."

I explained to her about Alyssa and Dr. Weirdbeard. Sancha told me that my teacher was funny, and Alyssa was sad, and perhaps lacking in self-esteem. She told me about her life in Holland, and some of it sounded familiar and the rest was completely new and weird.

For the next few weeks, me and Sancha played together every night. We leveled up quite a bit, and even when we weren't actively questing it was nice to have someone to talk to. We started a guild, a private one just for the two of us. Someday we might let other people join. Someday.

More than anything else, I wanted to meet Sancha. I mean in real life. I wanted to fly to Holland and live in her parents' basement. Over and over I told myself I would do it. I would get up and go. Sancha was the most interesting person in the world.

Sometimes I thought about Dr. Weirdbeard. I wondered if, when it came to Sancha, I was accepting reality or not. Mostly I didn't care. In the real world, Holland is only a plane ride away, but I can't afford a ticket. That's reality for you.

The other day I walked by the teacher's lounge again. Dr. Weirdbeard sat in there with the rest of them. He drank coffee. He talked a lot and waved his hands. All the other teachers laughed at his jokes. He said words like "semantics" and "Jean-Luc Godard." Dr. Weirdbeard had become the center of some strange little world that existed only inside the teachers' lounge. He seemed happy. Even though I knew I could never be part of that world, I felt happy for him, too.

That same day, I saw Alyssa in the school parking lot. Alyssa had gotten back with Troy, so she never talked to me anymore. I watched her from out the window on the school bus where I sat alone. She didn't look like the Alyssa I used to know. She didn't look like the girl who focused all her rage and hate to kill the Orc Lord with her Hell Slash. She looked small, and sad, and far away.

I watched as she and Troy got into his Chevy. He stood outside while she sat down in the passenger seat, and he slammed shut the door, and she disappeared. I mean completely. Like she'd never existed. Like she'd never shared a seat with me on the bus, like we'd never played video games, like we'd never kissed on the football field. Alyssa wasn't in Emoland, but she wasn't in the real world, either. She was somewhere else. Somewhere lonely. I imagine her sometimes, sitting in her room. She looks at the walls. She looks at the windows. She wonders if they open or if they're painted shut. She tries to remember what the wind feels like on her face.

An Invisible Place Above Us

Sometimes I think back to when we were kids and played doctor in your tree house out back. I'd pull up my shirt, and you'd unzip, and we'd look at each other and say the words we learned on TV doctor shows, words like "cancer" and "Zoloft" and "cerebral palsy." Showing ourselves to each other made me feel a certain way—not sexual, not even in love, but some sort of proto-emotion that might eventually have evolved into love. You stared at the flat place where one day I would grow breasts, and you said "lupus." You said "hepatitis," "Paxil" and "lymphoma."

We were always friends and very close. I joined your soccer league and karate class. We played video games and rode our bikes up and down the block until after dark. I remember how you'd look up at all the stars and tell me secrets. You wanted to be a pilot someday. You had a hamster once, but it died when you stopped feeding it. You fell in love with some bitch named Emily.

Back in those days, there was nobody I wanted to murder more than Emily. I wanted to put out her eyes with the stupid charms from her bracelet. I wanted her to choke on her own pom-poms. I wanted to see bloodstains on her chalk-white Keds.

On the night the two of you finally made it official at the homecoming dance, I took a Solo cup of punch to the girls' restroom and sat on a toilet. I poured vodka into the punch and drank, and when I ran out of punch, I just drank vodka. Sometime later I woke up in the dark with my face pressed against the cold tile floor. Everything smelled like piss. Even my hair smelled like piss.

Once she got her fangs into you, it was like you left me behind. There was no more hanging out in your bedroom on Saturday afternoons. No more reading comics and watching bad Samurai movies on TV. At night I'd lie in bed alone and think about how we used to play doctor when we were kids. I wanted to show myself to you again. I wanted to put my face in your lap and keep it there until you belonged to me.

Sometimes I would tell myself, "I'm sinking into shit. I'll just keep sinking deeper and deeper until I can't breathe anymore." I kept saying it until the night you and Emily had an argument. It happened in front of everyone on New Year's. You yelled until sticky lumps of spittle flew out of the corners of your mouth. Everybody at the party got quiet and watched. Afterward your face was so red, and you wouldn't look anyone in the eye.

"This is perfect," I said out loud to myself. "This is a gift from fucking God."

I brought you a drink. We talked on a couch in the corner, just the two of us, and it was like everyone else just faded into static. Later we walked outside in the dark and snow. You held my hand. We watched white flakes fall from some invisible place above us and pile up around our feet, like the world was creating itself, like it was becoming new again. We saw a leafless tree iced-over by the storm. We stood beneath it and stared as it swayed and creaked in the wind, and you asked me how it could survive, all covered in ice.

"Let's run away together," I said. "Let's go someplace new. Somewhere just the two of us. Fuck. Let's leave the whole planet. Let's just fly up in the sky someplace where we can be alone. That's what I've always wanted, just to be alone with you forever."

I moved close, put my head to your chest, felt snowflakes on your coat melt against my cheek. I thought something was about to happen between us, something I'd waited a long time for, something I'd earned. But when I looked up, you were just staring back at the house. You didn't put your tongue in my mouth or run away with me because you were still caught up with that bitch Emily.

I stayed out in the snow for a while after you went back inside. I looked at the tree again. It didn't even look like a real tree anymore. It was the ghost of a tree, a corpse. I slipped my hand out of its glove and touched an ice-covered twig, noticed how the crystal felt smooth and cold. I wanted to build a miniature treehouse in the branches, high up in the air. I'd fill it with two tiny snow people, and I'd shape the snow on their backs into wings. And they'd stay up there all winter, frozen and perfect and hidden away. And when spring came and melted the ice, their souls would live on and fly up into the sky, into that secret place where nobody is ever alone.

Age of Darkness

You know how sometimes you can just feel it when something is wrong? Like Spider-man and his spider senses. You get the tingles. Well, something like that happend to me when I was fourteen. I woke up one morning and felt it. The *wrongness*. It was a school day, but the light streaming into my bedroom was way too bright. Maybe that's what tipped me off. I stayed under the blankets for a while, wondering why nobody had woken me up. Eventually, I rolled out of bed and set off to figure out what was going on. I found mom in the living room. Mom acted weird. Instead of making breakfast like always, she just slumped on the couch and cried. I tried to talk to her, but she kept crying. I ran to my parents' bedroom to get dad. He was gone. And then I understood. Dad was gone.

✼ ✼ ✼

The dumbest thing about my parents' divorce was how I felt so embarrassed about it. I mean, obviously, it wasn't my fault. Even at fourteen I was old enough to understand it had nothing to do with me. It was some weird emotional thing between them, some weird resentment thing. But still I felt—deep down where I couldn't hide from it—that I was to blame, that I'd done something to drive him off, or even that something I could do might bring him back. And of course this was the same bullshit that every child of divorce dreams up. Regardless, I felt terrible. Ashamed. I felt like I'd failed, and no matter what, I would continue failing forever.

The thing I did to make myself feel better was play a lot of video games. The point of video games is to kill. Tap the blue button—kill. Press the red button—murder-death-kill. In those days, me and my closest friends were a hard bunch of killers. They all had better games than me, and their parents, not surprisingly, had more disposable income than mine. At some point, I guess when all of us were in junior high, my friends upgraded to the shiny new 16-bit consoles. This would have been in the early 1990s. My best friend had a Sega Genesis, and it looked like a hot-rod spaceship. I'd go over to his house, and we'd stay up all night playing Super Thunder Blade, Revenge of Shinobi and Phantasy Star II. Then I'd go home and power up my Nintendo. It was from the 80s and shaped like a brick. It mostly played lame games like Kid Icarus and Kirby. But I did have one really great one. A classic. A game called Ninja Gaiden. It's the kind that turns nice boys from the suburbs into cold-eyed assassins. The kind that sticks with you long after you beat it. The kind that becomes a part of you, and in some ways you're better for it, and in other ways you're worse.

* * *

Ninja Gaiden is a story of revenge. It was one of the earliest games to feature cinematic cutscenes between levels, and through them you learn how your father met a stranger in a field one rainy night, and they fought, and your father lost. Ninja Gaiden is a game where you are driven, in the words of the narrator, to discover "With whom did my father have a duel and lose? For what reason did he fight and die?" You accomplish this mostly by running forward and ninja-slashing anyone who gets in your way.

Ninja Gaiden begins on an ordinary city street, but as the game progresses, the settings and characters become more exotic and magical. You discover secret mountain hideouts. Duplicitous government agents. Forbidden ruins. Undead things with skull heads. Mine shafts. Weird stuff like ninjas in the Amazon jungle. Homunculi. Demon statues. Occult temples. Fathers and sons. The night of rebirth.

Something else you should know is that the game is frustratingly difficult. Like the designers purposefully placed enemies in the most inconvenient locations. Like to complete many of the jumps, you must leap from the exact right spot, and even if you do it perfectly, something completely out of your control—a stray shuriken or kamikaze bird—might appear out of nowhere to fuck everything up.

One night not long after my dad left, I stayed up and played the game until morning. I kept my door shut and turned the volume down low so mom wouldn't hear. I made it all the way to an extremely difficult level near the end of the game, where you climb this mountain in the jungle. But then I came to one particularly frustrating jump. I kept trying and failing, growing angrier with each death. And then, miraculously, after about my millionth death, I did manage to land it. I ran forward, feeling unstoppable, until some random ninja bumped me off the side of the mountain. I had to restart the level from the beginning. And after I worked my way back to that same jump, I couldn't get past it again. I died and died and kept on dying. I wondered why any asshole programmer would make a game so hard. I wondered why my friends all had the cool new games and I was stuck with this trash. I wondered why my father left without saying a word—no explanation, no apology. I wondered why, whenever I asked my mom about it, she'd just change the subject or sigh and tell me it was too complicated for me to understand. That always pissed me off. I was four-fucking-teen years old, and I could understand any fucking thing in the world. I yanked the controller out of the Nintendo and slung it against the wall as hard as I could manage— which turned out to be pretty hard. Somehow my mom slept through the noise. I sat on the bedroom floor and tried to calm down, catch my breath. After a while I started worrying that I'd busted the controller. I knew my mom well enough to know she wouldn't pay for a new one. I crept over to where it had fallen. Picked it up. And it was fine. Those old Nintendo controllers were damn near indestructible.

* * *

It didn't take long for my life to settle into a comfortable routine. I'd come home after school and go to my room ostensibly to do homework but actually to play Ninja Gaiden. Later mom would call me to dinner. I could remember a time when she would actually cook—like real, honest-to-God food—but all she did anymore was heat up soups. I don't have any particular problem with soups. Some soups are quite good, like that egg stuff they give you at Chinese restaurants. But soups every night … I don't know. It gets depressing after a while. Mom usually would make an effort to talk to me, ask me about my day at school. I never had much to say. Eventually we'd shut up and eat our soups. We shared a room and table but inhabited vastly different worlds.

After a few months, dad started calling sometimes at night, and those phone calls were every bit as awkward as my dinners with mom. I didn't know what to say to him anymore. I found out he was living in a studio apartment across town. He invited me to visit, but I really didn't want that. I didn't want to see him schlepping around some gross little room. I mean, he was my dad. I didn't want to feel sorry for him.

Sometimes—when the receiver was pressed against my ear and we didn't have anything to talk about, and the only noise I'd hear was the faint hum from the electronics of the phone—I would think to ask him why he left. Just why. Seriously, why? It was all I wanted to know anymore. But of course I never asked. I couldn't. Sometimes the simplest things are impossible.

* * *

Ninja Gaiden has a villain—the Jaquio. Even as a kid, I thought it was a weird name. I didn't know what business some Frenchy guy had with a bunch of ninjas. Anyway, the Jaquio is extremely evil. He uses mind control on your father—who is alive after all—and forces you to fight to the death. He conspires to resurrect an ancient demon and usher in a new age of darkness. You fight and kill the Jaquio, but you're too late. The moon eclipses the sun. The demon rises from the dead. It looks like one of those H.R. Giger monsters from the Alien movies, sort of like a fetus, some terrible, slimy, half-born thing. And like all video game bosses, there is a trick to killing it. You must chop off its head and tail to expose its weak spot. You must plunge your dragon sword into its heart and guts. That's what kills it, the way you tear it apart from the inside. It's disgusting but you do it. You do whatever it takes to survive, to win. You still believe winning is possible, even in the real world. Killing the demon is your last task before beating the game. You are rewarded with a short movie to wrap up the story. The ninja stands atop the mountain. His long work is finished. I believe, in the end, he finds happiness—though it's hard to say for sure because video game narratives weren't very sophisticated back then. I like to imagine he's happy. The ninja knows his struggle was not in vain. He saved the world. He made peace with his father.

* * *

I probably sound like all I ever did back then was play video games, like they were my life and I had nothing else. That's not entirely true. I mean, it was true for a while after my dad left, but it didn't stay that way forever. It most definitely wasn't true before the divorce, because dad never would have let me play so much. I guess he was pretty athletic when he was younger, so he always bugged me to play football or basketball, even though I didn't like sports and wasn't good at them.

Sometimes in the fall, he would take mom and me hiking. I remember one time we followed a trail up a hill on the Natchez Trace. I was pretty young then, and I kept calling it a mountain, even though it was actually just a big hill. At the top, the trees gave way to a sun-drenched meadow dotted with purple and yellow flowers. I asked my parents if we could leave the trail and walk through the grass, and they smiled and said it would be fine, and I stood between them, holding hands, and we walked through the grass, and a breeze set the whole meadow rising and falling like waves in the ocean, and—on the whole—it's about the nicest day I can remember spending with my mother and father, back in the distant past when they loved each other and loved me, too.

* * *

One night, maybe six months after dad left, I ate soup for dinner with mom like always, and we made our usual bullshit small talk. I wondered if dad would call. Sometimes he did and sometimes he didn't. The uncertainty left me tense. I waited for it all through dinner, but the phone didn't ring, and actually I was relieved because I didn't have anything new to tell him. I remember mom carried some dirty bowls to the sink, and I was about to go to my room to play Ninja Gaiden, and that's when the phone rang. Dad sounded different that night. There were no awkward silences. Dad talked and talked. He told a long story about his job, and I didn't understand much of it except that the point of the story was his boss was an asshole. He said it over and over, that his boss was an asshole. I'd heard people cuss before—lots of people—but I'd never heard words like that from my dad. He abruptly changed the subject. He asked about mom. He told me he still cared about her. He got all choked up about it.

"Tell your mother I love her, OK?" he said. "Can you tell her that? Can you do that for me?"

"I guess," I said. "Sure. I guess I can do that."

"Good," he said. "You're a good boy. Tell her how much I love her. Tell her I love her as much as I did the day we met. Or more. Fuck. Tell her I love her more today than I've ever loved her. Tell her I know I was wrong and I'm sorry. Tell her I love her, and I don't want anything in the world anymore but to be with her, again, like we used to when we were a real family."

"I don't know," I said. "I don't know if I can say all that."

"Please son," he said. "Please do this for your father, OK? Please just be a good boy and do this one thing."

"I don't know," I said.

I listened to my dad sob for a while before I hung up. I stood there in the kitchen, staring at the phone. I hoped it would never ring again. I thought if it rang, I would knock it off the wall. I would stomp it and smash it and watch it die.

* * *

That night, I locked my bedroom door, switched on the Nintendo and threw myself into Ninja Gaiden. I lashed out with my dragon sword and magic shuriken. I killed everything. I killed punks on the street. I killed hermits who hid their faces behind robes. I killed ninjas. I killed devil dogs and skeleton men. I killed all those damn birds that fuck you up when you try to jump. I killed and killed and didn't stop. The killing helped me. I killed my demon-possessed father. I killed the Jaquio. I killed the beast who reawakened after eons of dreamless sleep. And when everything that required killing had, at last, been killed, a peculiar feeling overtook me. I felt as if I had been walking all my life down a narrow hallway, until suddenly a door opened, and for the first time in my life I saw the sky. I understood that my old life was over, replaced by a new one springing forth like a blast of neon pixels from the screen. I dropped the controller. I turned away from the game and peered out the window, saw the same lawn and driveway and trees I'd been looking at for my entire life. Only on this night, the landscape seemed infused by an unseen power. I looked down at my hands. Didn't recognize them. What kind of person was I becoming? A good man? A bad one? I yearned, like the ninja-hero of my game, to walk the earth and conquer foes, to discover lost places and secret wisdom. The journey would be long. It would take me far from my cozy bedroom and my parents' failing love. I saw no reason to delay. All that remained was to press start.

* * *

The ninja lowered his sword. His labors at last had ended. He stood atop the mountain and marveled to have survived the night, marveled to see the darkness give way not to sunlight but something brighter.

MICHELLE & ROCKETS

All the way to the beach Michelle talked about rocket-propelled grenades. I took the highway north from Kona through miles of volcanic desolation. This was not the Hawaii pictured in tourist brochures. This was desert, where bare rock—red and black—thrust skyward like jagged rows of teeth. This was wispy yellow grasses persisting among stone. This was no fantasy, no dream vacation. We had come to a land where wind sang lonely songs through the crags.

I took my eyes off the road to watch Mauna Kea towering in the distance. The reddish cone rose toward heaven before disappearing, finally, into a bank of clouds, ensuring the summit and whatever laconic wisdom could be found there would remain hidden.

"I like the practicality of the rocket-propelled grenade," Michelle said, shaping an outline of the device with her hands in the air. "Long range. We can stand on a rooftop down the street. Fire it through a goddamn window."

"This is serious," I said. "If they catch you trying to buy one, they'll put you away. Federal penitentiary. Lockdown. No joke."

"I know people," she said. "People who acquire things. Nobody's going to prison. Anyway fear is no reason to stop. Cowardice. Our work is important. We have principles."

"RPGs are big," I said. "They're not something you can stuff in a handbag. What'll you do? Sling it over your shoulder and take a stroll through Times Square?"

Michelle bit her bottom lip and stared out the window at the mountain, as if in consultation.

"Explosives then. C4 or something. As long as it's military grade. That way people take us seriously. If we throw together some DIY MacGyver bullshit from rubber bands and light bulbs, everybody writes us off as kooks."

"We are kooks."

"Nobody writes off ordnance."

Getting to the beach required almost an hour's drive through wasteland. Despite this, we arrived to find it packed. And for good reason. Several hundred yards of white sand. Cerulean water with low surf. Black lava rock to the north with coconut trees rising beyond, and further still the cantilevered walls of some Richie-Rich resort. A postcard image and it gave me the creeps. It seemed too perfect for this world, too soft and beautiful. Something had to give. Sharks? Landmines? What?

"Paradise." Michelle lay on a towel, her skin glistening with sweat. "This is it. This is the real shit."

I worked sunscreen onto my face and shoulders. Michelle went without, hoping for a darker tan. Later she slipped her swim goggles over her black hair, wore them like a necklace. We held hands on the way to the ocean. The water felt like ice, and after the heat of the sand the cold came as a sudden, shocking relief. We waded past kids riding the surf on bodyboards. Distant snorkelers explored a line of rocks penetrating the surface. I splashed around in shallow water.

"Let's go farther," Michelle said.

"Here is fine." I floated on my back.

The sky was clear blue but for a few wisps of high-altitude clouds. I rose and fell with the waves. Michelle stared out to sea.

"Explosions," she said. "That's what we need. The symbolism is right. Some noise to wake people up."

"Maybe they're already awake. Things are getting better. Iraq. The war is over, troops are home."

"They're still getting the fuck shot out of them in Afghanistan. Anyway this is bigger than the war. Look at the economy. The whole system of politics is breaking down. Look at how a couple of rich douchebags run everything. We're not even a real democracy anymore. Election Day? That's just a show. A ritual. The douchebags run things now."

Michelle took a few strokes out to sea.

"Let's check out those rocks," she said. "I want to see what's down there."

"Later," I said. "I'm tired. And it's nice here."

"I've been thinking about targets." She kicked her legs to keep her head above water. "Any big bank would be fine, but Wall Street is where it's at. Send an RPG into the stock exchange. Wham. Ain't no clearer message."

"Explosions kill people."

"Timing," she said. "Do it when no one's home. In the wee hours. Shut it down. Really shut it down. Not like those kids chanting slogans at Zuccotti Park. You saw where that got us, right? Nowhere. Now's the time for action."

I floated. Tasted saltwater. Observed the sky for portents.

"I'm going back," I said, hiking my thumb at the sand. "Drying out."

"Mr. Excitement." She pressed the goggles to her eye sockets. "I'm heading for those rocks."

The goggles transformed her into an alien, albeit a beautiful one, with long limbs and sharp features. I knew every curve, every secret, her dreams for the future, stories from her childhood, but somehow I didn't know her at all. She turned and kicked, reached an arm toward the horizon, each stroke pulling her to deeper waters.

I waded to shore, left a trail of footprints to my towel. The sun baked my salt-covered body. I heard the roar of surf, yelps and laughter of children. Somewhere in the water Michelle held her breath, dove deep. I sensed the weight of the sky above me, the entire planet behind my back. I felt like a small thing between them.

Voices crowded my head, demanded to know if I was in or out, how much violence I could stomach, how far the bonds of love would bend before breaking. I considered Michelle and rockets, explosions and severed limbs, high ideals, the depths of depravity.

"Where will it end?" I asked the ocean, the clouds, the mountain. And the universe replied, as always, with the immense silence of earth and sky.

Who are you? I'm a bear

Once I got my hands on a copy of the game, I pretty much figured I'd drop out of life for good. And, let me tell you, things on that front went swell. Like I kept the lights off. Like I increased my Dorito consumption to approximately ninety-nine percent of my diet. Like my character in the game had a bald head, and I thought maybe I'd shave mine so we'd have more in common.

I made sure to keep my phone on silent. Every couple days, I'd check the messages. One day my parents called. I took note of it and went back to the game. And I kept thinking the next call would be from you, or you'd send a text or something. I kept right on thinking it. Some mornings I'd read the news online. I heard about the guy who shot all those people. And how the price of gas went crazy, but everybody kept buying it. And how the national debt exploded, and all the economists said we were fucked.

"Typical," I said aloud in my empty apartment. Ostensibly I spoke to myself, but really, I was talking to you.

The best story was about some vortex of garbage in the Pacific Ocean. All the shit people dump out there—tons of stuff but mostly sludge and plastic—gets funneled by the currents, and now the patch is hundreds of square miles, and it just spins around and feeds itself while sunlight breaks down the plastics into deadly chemicals. I imagined telling you about the garbage vortex, and, in my head, you told me that somewhere in there was a metaphor for our relationship.

After most of a week, I left the apartment to pick up some Netflix movies at the mailbox. The internet told me they would be there, but when I opened the mailbox they weren't there. Neither, I might add, was any correspondence from you. All I got was a sheet of coupons for some Arby's sandwiches and an oil change.

"Hey mister," said somebody on the sidewalk behind me. It sounded like a girl's voice, but after I spun around, I saw it was a boy, maybe thirteen years old. He wore a T-shirt with a skull and dragon and some chains. Another kid trailed behind him, several years younger. The younger kid wore a scarf around his neck even though it was August and the sun was baking hot.

"Hey mister, buy me some smokes," said the older kid, holding out a ten-dollar bill and nodding to a gas station across the street.

I considered buying the kid some smokes.

"Cigarettes are for pussies," I said.

I turned back to the mailbox and closed the lid.

"Hey mister, watch my brother for a second, will you?" he said.

I opened my mouth to tell the kid—nicely—to go fuck himself, but he was already tearing across the street, flagging down some random guy outside the gas station.

I looked down at his brother. The kid looked up at me. He adjusted his scarf and smiled, his tongue flicking through the space where one of his front teeth used to be.

"I'm a robot," he said.

"No you're not," I said.

He held his arms stiff at the elbows and swung them mechanically from his shoulders.

"Beep-beep. I'm a robot."

"You should rat out your brother to your mom. Tell her he smokes. It'll be funny."

"Mom lets him smoke."

"Does she let you smoke?"

"Smoking makes my head feel funny."

"Jesus Christ," I said.

"I'm a robot," he said, rotating his torso while swinging his arms.

"I'm a bear," I said.

The kid stopped swinging his arms. He looked at my face like it was a crossword puzzle.

"You don't look like a bear."

"I hibernate," I said. "I sleep in a cave. It's nice in my cave, and cool, and when I'm in it nobody bothers me, and none of the bad stuff in the world matters because I'm safe and alone underground."

"Grrr," he said. "I'm a bear."

"Someday humans will be extinct. Someday bears will rule the world."

The kid made claws out of his hands and raked the air.

"Grrr. I ate all the people!"

"If there are any cities left, with houses, the bears will move into them," I said. "And the bear cities will be pretty chill because the bears won't have guns or nuclear bombs."

"I'm a nuclear bear!" he said.

Just then I saw his brother crossing back across the street.

"Remember," I said. "Bears don't smoke."

I turned and walked to my apartment. I reached for the doorknob but paused because I noticed the flowers some landscaper had planted in the dirt beside the door. The flowers were white and violet, and a bee buzzed as it flew figure eights around a blossom, and I thought maybe instead of going back into my apartment I'd take a walk, or drive out to the country for a hike, somewhere remote and quiet, where the trees grow to be giants and an overpowering scent of pine infuses the air, where the only human noises would be the whisper of my breath and the rhythmic drumming of my shoes against the earth, and where—if I crouched under a bush and kept silent—I might see a family of bears as they roamed in the cool of the forest. But instead of doing anything like that I twisted the knob and went inside to unpause my game, and I had a very fine time, not that you care. You've made it abundantly clear you don't care.

Love in the Time of the Etruscans

Some nights instead of sleeping I stay online. Some nights I read on Wikipedia about the Aztecs or Etruscans. Or I look at pictures of people having sex. Those are the good nights—but there are bad nights, too. Nights when I lurk on the timeline of the girl who used to love me, and I see pictures of her in bars, surrounded by friends smiling and making faces for the camera, and she leans on the shoulder of some guy with impressive stubble, some guy who looks ruggedly handsome in a way I never will. Some nights I type instant messages but don't click *send*.

How to Write an Emotionally Resonant Werewolf Novel

I.

Purchase a large notebook.

2.

Think deeply about every werewolf story you know—every book, TV show or movie. Ask yourself what makes your werewolf story different. Do you have anything new to say about werewolves? Does anybody? What even is the point? Maybe instead of writing, you should curl up on the couch and watch Netflix. Maybe you should go back to sleep.

3.

But what if you can't sleep? What if your eyes are bloodshot from not sleeping? What if you can't even remember the last time you hungered or thirsted? Maybe there's something alive inside you, and it wants to come out. Maybe it's a story. A werewolf story.

4.

What you need to do is try on the werewolf's shoes, so to speak. Imagine for a moment you really are a werewolf. A secret werewolf. You commute to work every day in a Hyundai, make small talk with co-workers, meet deadlines and quarterly earnings goals—and all the while, nobody has any idea. Nobody suspects the truth. No one sees the animal.

5.

Don't bother picking a theme. Your theme is: werewolf! Emotionally resonant werewolf, no less. The theme is a man who hides the rage inside himself, a man brought low by a mocking and indifferent world. The theme is a sudden snapping, a release of repressed energy. The theme is man becoming animal. The impenetrable wilderness of the heart.

6.

Pretend to avoid obvious werewolf clichés while actually exploiting them.

7.

In an emotionally resonant werewolf novel, choosing a villain will be difficult. Typically, the werewolf plays the villain, but this does not have to be the case. Maybe the werewolf is both victim and victimizer. Maybe the villain is the woman who lied to him. Who hurt him. The woman who broke a sacred vow. Maybe there is no villain. Maybe there's nothing but anger. Maybe all the world's a stage, and you and I are merely werewolves.

8.

Think about characters. There will, obviously, be a werewolf. And the werewolf is you. And the werewolf needs someone to love. Someone to betray him. Maybe her name is Jillian. Maybe Jillian was your wife. Maybe you loved her once, and maybe she loved you back. Maybe none of it matters anymore. Maybe it all happened a long time ago.

9.

Think more about these characters. Think about their weirdness and contradictions. What motivates your werewolf? Why did his wife leave him? She didn't simply abandon him out of the clear blue sky. What did he do to push her away? Why did he stop listening? Admit to yourself that your transformation from man to animal was a long, slow process. Glacial. Like the sluggish drift of tectonic plates.

10.

The first chapter must make a promise to the reader. Promise a man will transform into a beast. His flesh will sprout a thick coat of fur. Teeth will lengthen into fangs. Hands will curl into claws. Promise blood and fury. This next part is important—never, ever break a promise. A broken promise can rip a man's heart out. So don't. Don't rip anybody's heart out.

11.

Begin writing.

12.

Continue writing.

13.

When you are too exhausted to go on, bear down and write some more.

14.

Pause for a moment to consider how ridiculous you will sound when attempting to pitch your emotionally resonant werewolf novel to an agent.

15.

Think about all the people who have hurt you. Think most of all about the girl. Jillian. The one you loved. The one who lied. Remember what it was like in the beginning. Remember what the touch of her lips and skin awoke inside you. Remember what it meant to hold her. To rest your head on the pillow you shared. To gaze into the infinity of her eyes. To sleep with her beneath a soft blanket, submerging yourself in a sea of warmth and love.

16.

Write it true, but write it slanted. Write so the details are fictional but arranged in such a way to make the reader feel the things you have felt. What you're aiming for is emotional truth. By the time your readers reach the end, they should know you more intimately than your own wife ever did. Just write your damn heart out. And people will read it. And they will know.

17.

Fiddle around with third-person and omniscient points of view, but be aware you will inevitably revert to the first person. The reader must see through the eyes of the wolf.

18.

Think back to the day—so long ago—when you and Jillian rented a cabin in a state park. And you hiked for hours on a warm afternoon in the springtime. And the flowers smelled nice, and you talked and laughed, and at one point you got lost, a little, and you were still in the woods at nightfall. And the shadows of the forest lengthened until there was nothing else, nothing but shadows. You heard a rustling in the bushes off the trail, and she clung to you, and you told her not to be afraid, you'd find your way out of the woods, you were almost out already, you could feel it. And she smirked, and in the shadows her green eyes shone like magic, and she said "Don't worry about me, babe. I'm the wildest thing out here."

19.

Bring your characters to a point of crisis. The novel must lead them there, but slowly, along a winding path, dropping breadcrumbs all the way. Don't telegraph your punches. You will know you have succeeded if the reader finds the crisis both surprising and inevitable. The girl must leave the boy. It will be ugly. Now is not the time to flinch from hard truths. Make her hurt him. You can do it. You're in charge. You're the writer. Make her twist the metaphorical knife. He will bleed. Warm blood gushes, pumped from his still-beating heart. She will betray him. He will rage. Crisis. Climax. She must destroy him.

20.

The night of the full moon. A peculiar feeling. You shudder, skin tingling as if you are cold. But you are not cold. You burn. The wolf is inside you. The wolf wants out. Skin explodes into fur. Teeth and fingers sharpen into knives. Scream. Howl. The wolf returns. Once again it has found its way into the realm of men, passing through a doorway in a heart seething with hate. The wolf smiles toothily. The wolf always comes back.

21.

Run through the forest. Sniff the air. Catch the meaty scent of flesh. Find lovers naked among the trees. Jaws clamp. Screams. Clawing. Tearing. Bones snap. Skin. Hair. Excrement. Vomit. Now blood paints the leaves of the forest floor. The wolf licks his grinning lips. Soon the forest is full of men. They hunt you. They carry guns. No matter. You tear through them. Rip throats. Slit bellies to spill their guts. You stand atop a pile of bodies. So much blood. Howl.

Howl at your goddess the moon. Sniff the air. Now you smell her. Her. Jillian. You run, nose to the ground, tracking. You snort. Laugh. You find her. A small house on the edge of the forest. A locked door. Sniff the air. She's alone. Bash the door to splinters. There she is. Screaming. Tongue lolls out of your mouth. Drooling. Long hair. Short dress. She will taste sweet. You lunge, opening your jaws wide to fit your teeth around her throat, to rip it out and feel the warm spray of blood, when—abruptly, perplexingly—you freeze. You loom above her, breathing hot, wolfish breath. You look at her. Jillian. You know her. You remember. And you realize what you have to do. The wolf turns away. The wolf flees into the darkened woods. You run and run. You run until you're not a wolf anymore but a man—naked and alone. You fall. You curl among wet leaves. Not a howl any longer but a whimper. You think about the things you did. The things you almost did. You think about what you were becoming, and you are sorry, and you are small, and you are afraid.

22.

Remove your hands from the keyboard. Lean back in your chair. Smoke a cigarette. The smoke tastes delicious. Know that you loved her once, and she loved you, too. Now it's over. She's gone. And it's OK. People leave, and it hurts, and this is life. You learned something. You wrote it all down. The work is finished. And it's good. Exhale slowly. Rest now. Close your eyes. Even werewolves need to sleep.

Death Cult

I

I used to stare at this girl Carmen in Sunday school. The teacher would say words like sin and Jesus and grace, and I just couldn't stop looking at Carmen, at the white tip of cleavage peeking out of her dress. I think maybe I loved her. She didn't love me back. I know this because in all our years of Bible classes she spoke fewer words to me than I've written in this sentence. I failed at love. When I saw her sometimes, from far away, I felt like there was no use in wanting anything. At these times, I'd look to the clouds and ask God why, after all my prayers, why?

And then, around the time I turned sixteen, I abruptly stopped failing. I remember the day it happened. The moment. Me and my friend-for-life Daryl ate together at a long table in our church's fellowship hall. It was Sunday, and the preacher had finished his sermon, and the whole congregation had packed into the hall for a potluck dinner. The room was crowded and smelled of fried chicken. Daryl held up a spoon and made airplane noises. He was, objectively, too old to play airplane with his utensils, but for as long as I'd known him, he'd dreamed of one day becoming a fighter pilot, and he took the dream quite seriously. To be Daryl's friend—his true friend, as I was—one had to make certain allowances.

Daryl was strafing a pile of mashed potatoes when Carmen sat down beside me. Carmen of dark hair and pale skin. Carmen of my private dreams. She asked for a book of matches. And she'd come to the right guy: I was an acolyte, meaning I lit the altar candles before Sunday services. From a young age I'd been tasked with carrying light into the sanctuary.

Carmen told me to meet her outside with the matches. She made eye contact, cleared a lock of hair away from her face, then stood up and left. I looked at Daryl. He lowered his spoon and gazed thoughtfully at it for a moment.

"You'd better do what she wants," he said. "If you don't, she'll probably murder you."

"I might like it if she murdered me."

"Not for long you wouldn't," he said.

"I mean if she just murdered me a little."

I left the fellowship hall to snatch a book of matches from the shelf in the narthex where I stored my robe and candle lighter. Then I caught up with Carmen on the stone steps outside the church.

"Thanks, dork," she said, rolling her eyes as I sat beside her. She held a cigarette casually between two fingers. "Hand them over."

But I had something better in mind. Something cinematic. I opened the book and tore out a cardboard match. In the instant it took to scrape the match head against the striker, I prayed silently to God for it to light on my first try. The miniature torch sizzled and burned, and I held it out to Carmen, who slid the tip of her cigarette into the fire. I shook out the match and tossed it down the steps, and for a moment we watched the blackened and twisted thing smolder.

She smoked.

I struggled to think of something interesting to say.

I expected her to tell me to buzz off. It's the kind of thing eighteen-year-old women sometimes said to sixteen-year-old boys like me. Instead she showed me her tattoo. She stretched out her left leg and pulled up her skirt, lifted it past her calf, her knee, her thigh. A female skeleton clad in black robes brandished a scythe just below her hip.

"Santa Muerte," Carmen said. "The death saint. In Mexico there's a cult. It's huge. People pray to her."

"What people?" I said, mesmerized both by the death saint and Carmen's exposed leg.

"Criminals. Cartel assassins. They pray for Santa Muerte to bless them before they kill."

That's when I touched her. Without thinking I reached out, traced along the outline of the tattoo with my middle finger. Carmen's leg felt smoother than anything in my life.

"Do you believe?" I said. "Do you think she's real?"

My finger traveled to the apex of the scythe blade. The back of my hand brushed against the bunched fabric of her skirt. Carmen took a long time to answer.

2

After that, me and Carmen were pretty much inseparable. She wasn't my girlfriend or anything corny like that. She just liked me, and I liked her back, and—for a time—that was enough. In the beginning, our relationship revolved around her acknowledging my existence at school. Because of our age difference, we shared only one class. A football coach taught it, and for that reason it wasn't very rigorous. It left plenty of time for Carmen to tell me about the death cult.

"The highway from Tehuacán to Mexico City is littered with shrines to Santa Muerte," she said. "Before killing, an assassin must light a black candle. If the assassin fails to do this, if the ritual is not complete, then the assassin is nothing more than a common murderer."

"This is all very crazy," I said.

"Do you want to know a secret?" Before I could answer, she leaned forward to whisper. "I'm going to join the death cult. After graduation I'll catch a bus to El Paso, cross over into Juárez. I'll hook up with the cartel there. They'll take me to the mountains and train me to kill."

"Why would you want that?"

"Because everything sucks." She rolled her eyes like she'd made the most obvious point ever. "What? Should I take some crappy job as a waitress? Waste four years in college, spend the rest of my life in a cubicle? Maybe I should shit out some babies. Would you like that? Would you be more attracted to me if I was one of those cows shopping at Walmart?"

I tried to conjure an adequate reply.

"Fuck," she said, shrugging. "All I want is to kill people and get paid."

3

After school that day, I hung out at Daryl's house. Almost every day I'd either go to his place or he'd come to mine, but I preferred his house because it had better video games and junk food. His parents bought name brands. The real Ho Hos. Authentic Twinkies. Not the generic-value-choice knockoff shit like at my house.

Daryl sat at the desk in his bedroom and assembled a model aircraft. An Apache gunship—and a nice one, too, with a full suite of Hellfire missiles. I flipped through one of his *Soldier of Fortune* magazines and sat with my feet propped on the desk. The whole room smelled sweet like model glue. Really what I wanted was for Daryl to hurry up and turn on the Xbox so I could play *Call of Duty*.

"Carmen will probably fuck you this weekend," Daryl said.

"You don't know everything," I said.

"Dude, Carmen fucks everybody," he said. "And it's not even fair. I should be the first to have sex. I'm the cool one."

I flipped through some more pages in his Soldier of Fortune magazine. I looked at photos of people shooting AK-47s.

"If you want to impress Carmen, you'll have to be really good at sex," Daryl said. "Because she's had a lot of it. Seriously. A lot. You'll have to give it to her real hard and talk dirty. I hope you're ready. I heard she likes the weird stuff."

"Can we just play *Call of Duty*?"

"No, damn it," Daryl said. He threw down his tube of model glue, and some liquid splooged out of the nozzle and pooled on the desk. "I've got a big box of condoms under my bed, and you are going to take about a dozen of them, or else when Carmen seduces you, she'll give you human papillomavirus."

"Carmen is my girl," I said. "Don't you accuse her of carrying diseases."

"One in four people carry human papillomavirus," Daryl said. "Carmen's fucked all four of them—and their cousins. So take a condom, because I don't want you coming here next week spreading human papillomavirus all over my bedroom—or whatever other disease she has, probably herpes."

Eventually I accepted a condom, and Daryl fired up the Xbox. Almost every day we played *Call of Duty* for a few hours, so we'd become quite good at it. Me and Daryl made a solid team. He looked out for me, and I did the same for him. That afternoon we had everybody on the run and racked up a bunch of headshots and melee kills, as usual, but at one point we became separated, and some douchebag pinned me down with rocket-propelled grenades, and I thought I was toast until Daryl called in an airstrike.

"Boom," Daryl said, raising his hands like he'd scored a goal at the World Cup. "Airstrike, motherfucker!"

Partially he did it to save me, but partially he did it for the sheer joy of calling in an airstrike. Daryl really did love his airstrikes.

4

That weekend, I took Carmen to the movies in my father's Chevrolet. I'd tested for my license only a month earlier, and every time I drove into town I came close to ending up dead on the side of the road. On our date, I clenched the steering wheel, stared straight ahead and, in general, pretended like I knew what I was doing. Carmen played it cool. Whenever I blew past a stop sign or drove the wrong way down a one-way street, she just laughed and called me a madman.

At the theater we watched a Sam Raimi movie about demons and hell. During the opening credits I worked up the nerve to hold her hand. She smiled at me the way a girl might at a cute puppy or kid brother. Then she put her tongue in my mouth.

After the show I asked if she wanted to get something to eat. She told me she had something like that in mind. As soon as we got back into the Chevrolet, she started barking out directions.

"Turn here," she'd say abruptly. "Take this road."

Her instructions took us toward the outskirts of town, where nothing lived but trees and cows. Carmen ordered me to drive down a sketchy-looking chert road bordered by steep gullies. I drove slowly, rattled by potholes and fist-sized rocks. The woods closed in around us, and after the movie it was easy to imagine them crawling with murderers. And I mean the bad murderers—chainsaw-wielding lunatics with mutilated faces or hooks for hands. Eventually the trees opened into a field. Carmen told me to pull in. My headlights illuminated bushy crowns of waist-high grass as the car rolled to a stop.

"I love this place," she said.

All was quiet as we stared through the windshield. Points of light speckled the night sky.

"What do you want to do with your life?" she said. "I mean when you grow up."

"I don't know," I said. "Maybe I'll be a doctor or something. Maybe a scientist. I'm not actually sure what scientists do. But whatever it is, it's probably something I'd be good at."

"Jesus," she said. 'You'll be in college forever."

Carmen looked out the window for a long time before speaking again.

"I don't think being alive is as great as people say it is," she said. "I mean, life is shit, right? Life is crazy. It's all mixed up. Just look around you. Life should be more than this. Or less. Life should be simple."

As usual I didn't know what to say, but it didn't matter because Carmen put her tongue in my mouth. We made out more fiercely than before, grasping and groping. She didn't pull away until my taste buds ached.

"Technically," she said, reaching under my seat to pull a lever that sent me rolling backward, "what I'm about to do is illegal." She unbuttoned my jeans, eased down the zipper and fished around inside for my cock, which she then held firmly and pleasantly in the moonlight.

Now let me be clear. I wanted Carmen. I'd always wanted her. I'd jacked off to the idea of Carmen about a million times. But there in the car, face to face with the reality of Carmen—I don't know. I guess I freaked out or something. I was afraid she'd figure out I didn't know what I was doing, afraid of laughter or pity, afraid I'd ruin everything and she'd go back to treating me like just another stupid kid. Anyway I sat still and let her do whatever she wanted.

"Technically, you're jailbait," she said, stroking slowly up and down. A tiny bead of the early stuff seeped out, shining on the head of my penis like the ghost-white face of the death saint. Carmen leaned down to worship with her mouth.

5

The next Monday at school, my friends pumped me for details. I kept cool, didn't reveal too much. I knew if I told them the whole story with all the sexy details I'd lose my power over their imaginations. Daryl instigated. He came right out and asked if I'd fucked Carmen.

"We fooled around," I said, yawning theatrically.

"Sure," he said, "but did you fuck her?"

I smiled as if in on a secret joke.

"We fooled around."

It went on like that all day. I was the only guy among my friends making any sort of time with a girl—and a senior, no less. The situation was unprecedented. Miraculous. A gift of divine intervention.

"You're a braver man than I," Daryl said at the end of the day as we shouldered our backpacks and set off down the hallway.

"And better looking," I said.

"Don't get me wrong. I'm sure she's worth it."

"What are you even talking about?"

"You know. Her ex-boyfriends. All those guys who graduated like three years ago. Back when her nickname was 'jailbait.' Remember that guy—what's his name—Rat? And the dude whose face peeled off when he crashed his bike. And the twitchy one who punched Mrs. Grabowski because she kept bugging him for homework. Shit. Carmen's fucked a lot of guys. A bunch of violent assholes, really."

Blood drained from my face.

"She's experienced," I said, pretending to be the kind of guy who doesn't give a damn. "That's how I like them."

"Whatever," he said. "Just watch your back."

After school, I rode with Carmen to her house for the first time. She explained that her mom worked late, so we'd have a few hours to do whatever we wanted. I guess I expected her to live either in a trailer park or a Gothic cathedral, but her house turned out to be pretty normal. It was like my parents' place only a little bigger and in a swankier neighborhood.

"Get ready for heaven," she said on our way in.

I assumed she was making some clever reference to sex. She wasn't. She was referring to her mother's collection of ceramic angels, a host of which had conquered every available flat surface in the living room as completely as any born-again sinner's heart. Her mother had painted the walls blue and added sloppy-looking white clouds. Carmen told me her mom used to be pretty decent. But after Carmen's dad left, she started spending all her time at church and buying figurines.

"Vomit," she said.

Carmen's bedroom was what you might expect—punk rock posters, skateboarding stickers stuck to a computer desk, framed photos of suspicious-looking young men. Above her bed hung a black-light poster of the grim reaper, the same poster you could buy at any music store. But Carmen didn't call it the reaper. She called it the death saint.

She knelt at the foot of the bed, felt around underneath with her hands and pulled out a shoebox. Then we climbed onto the bed and sat Indian-style while she opened the box. Inside lurked two handguns. Carmen held them gingerly while showing them off, as if cradling a kitten or newborn child. Nickel plating gleamed in the dim light of her room, shining brightest on the iconographic filigree along the barrels. An engraved likeness of Santa Muerte peered out at us from the ivory hand grips.

"The guns of an assassin," Carmen said. "A real one. A member of the La Familia cartel. A man who lived to kill."

"Lived?"

"Mexican special forces caught up with him outside Veracruz. They'd tracked him for months. In the end, he killed five of them before they brought him down."

"How do you know?"

"It's what I heard," she said, shrugging. "I don't care if it's true."

She dared me to touch the weapons. I ran a finger along a cold barrel. It was impossibly smooth, and the oil from my skin left a sheen.

"Where did you get them?"

Carmen blushed—something I'd never seen before.

"From this guy I used to date. He traded a pound of weed to a Mexican he worked with building houses last summer. Rat could be an OK guy. He was a dick, don't get me wrong. But sometimes he was a nice dick."

She smiled softly as if remembering something pleasant from long ago.

"Well Jesus," I said too loudly. "Rat sure sounds like a fantastic guy. Why did you break up?"

Carmen rolled her eyes.

"It doesn't matter," she said.

"Sure it does," I said.

"Nothing matters," she said. "Nothing means anything. Grow up and accept it. Or don't. Remain a child forever. I don't care. Because nothing matters."

That's when Carmen told me she wanted to fuck. She placed the guns beside us on the bed, slithered atop me, pressed her mouth against mine, inserted her tongue. I tried to relax and get in the mood, but every time I closed my eyes I imagined Rat fingering a switchblade and laughing. When I opened them, I saw the guns.

I let Carmen grind on me until she realized something was missing. She asked me, "What the fuck is your fucking problem?" She accused me of not being attracted to her. I tried to explain but failed. Badly. She called me a pussy and a fag, in that order. I told her she wasn't worth the aggravation. She told me to get the fuck out. So I did. And gladly.

6

Weeks passed. I tried to forget about Carmen and failed at that, too. The school year ended. All the seniors graduated. I considered attending the ceremony and clapping for Carmen, but in the end I stayed home. Daryl went, and he told me how Carmen lifted her robe and flashed everybody. I tried not to care. I mean it: I really tried.

One warm night, I'd just finished jacking off to her memory when I heard a tap on my window. It was Carmen. It could have been no one else. She stood in the moonlight holding two silvery pistols. She asked me to come outside, to take a drive with her. Told me it was important.

Carmen took us back to where we'd spent the best moments of our brief relationship, to the clearing in the woods. On the way she explained her plan. She would leave home that night, place a note on her pillow for her mom to find in the morning. Carmen told me she was tired of all the bullshit. The pressure. Her mom constantly on her case about applying to college or finding a job or joining the goddamned Army. She told me she'd bought a bus ticket to Mexico. She would give up the only life she'd ever known to be reborn as a death-cult assassin.

When we arrived at the clearing, she turned off the motor. Headlights lit up a tree on the edge of the field.

"That's the one we'll shoot," she said. "Once you get used to it, it's easier than breathing. Once you get used to it."

I planted my feet in the wet grass. Carmen put a gun in my hand. She stood behind me as I took aim at the tree. She steadied my arm, whispered advice. Then she stepped back.

"Do it."

I pulled the trigger. A flash. One loud pop. The handgun jerked and hummed like a living thing. The bullet raced off somewhere in the thick of the woods. I dropped the gun, stepped away from it like I would have from a snake.

"Let me show you how it's done," Carmen said, scooping it from the ground and wiping away the dew with the bottom of her tank top.

She took a wide stance while holding a gun in either hand, raised both arms to shoulder height. She took two shots at once, scoring direct hits, the slugs burying themselves into the trunk with twin puffs of sawdust. She stepped back with one foot, pivoting her body and positioning her left hand so a pistol was a few inches south of her chin. Two shots. Two more hits. She spun forward, ducking low and catching herself in a partial crouch, one knee straight ahead of her, the other pressed into the damp earth. Two final shots. Two more explosions of trunk and bark.

"I'm a killer," Carmen said, the smoke from the barrels rising in a demonic halo. "I was born for this."

For now—and I expect forever—when I think back on Carmen I see her skin, pale white from twin muzzle flashes, and I remember the touch of her hands—cold and hard as the weapons she loved, icy mitts not unlike the skeletal talons of a goddess of eternal night.

I expected her to ask me to come to Mexico. I'd have done it. I'd have left everything, followed her anywhere. To Tijuana. Oaxaca. Even to hell. All she needed was to ask. Instead she wished me luck on becoming a scientist someday. She told me I'd make a good one because I was smart. Then she drove me home.

7

I read newspapers religiously for months after Carmen left, scoured the nation and world pages for any mention of the drug war. Though the body count rose daily, I found no evidence of her handiwork.

Time passed. I moved on with my life. I thought about Carmen a lot at first but later only occasionally. Eventually I dated other girls, compared them to her unfavorably. My remaining years of high school seemed the longest of my life. Then they ended, as all things do. As graduation neared, I remembered Carmen again with fierce intensity. I prepared for college and thought about the places life had taken us. It was an exciting time and a scary one. I found great solace in knowing that, somewhere in the humid Latin jungle, Carmen was slipping into a doomed man's villa through an unlocked balcony door, her heart racing but her hands calm, reassured by the comforting weight of her guns.

I graduated from high school with honors. I barely remember the ceremony. The valedictorian gave some bullshit speech. Caps were thrown. Me and Daryl stood in our crimson robes in the center of the gymnasium amid all the hugging and weeping. I told him how I'd applied to the big university down the road in Murfreesboro. He told me he'd been accepted to the United States Air Force Academy. I told him he'd make a great pilot. We promised to stay in touch no matter what. We shook hands and felt very adult about it.

"Someday there will be a war, and I'll be in it," he said. "Someday I'll kill a dictator by firing a single Hellfire missile. Boom. Easy as that. That's how simple life is. You can free a whole country with one Hellfire missile. Politicians and generals want you to believe it's more complicated than that. They muck everything up. But life, really, is very simple. You can save the goddamned world with one Hellfire missile."

8

All summer I looked forward to college. I told myself it would be easy, just another pit stop on the road to bigger and better things. In the fall I moved into a dormitory and started taking classes. College felt like high school and summer camp all rolled into one. It was new and weird, and I liked it, but it didn't really feel like the big deal that everyone had led me to expect. So naturally I was surprised when I returned home for Christmas and discovered I was no longer the same person I used to be. Already I felt my old life slipping away.

Not much important happened over the next few years. Nothing worth talking about. And then one morning—it must have been during my spring semester as a junior—I woke up in my dorm when the phone rang. I remember how the room looked very dark but the light outside the window was blinding. The call was from Daryl's younger brother. The brother had been just a kid the last time I saw him. At first, I didn't recognize his voice.

Daryl had died. He'd shot himself in the chest, and it was no accident. His brother told me the funeral would be held over the weekend. He remembered how close I used to be Daryl. He thought I'd want to know.

I put everything on hold to make it to the service, which was held in Hohenwald, about fifty miles from the town where we grew up. At the burial I recognized only Daryl's parents and brother, and even then only barely. I hadn't even talked to Daryl since the summer after high school. I didn't know him anymore. I felt out of place. More than that, actually. I felt like a voyeur. A liar.

A preacher said some words. Workers lowered a casket. People stood around for a while, then they left. Daryl's mother approached me, thanked me for coming. She looked lost, like she'd been kidnapped and dumped in a desert, like she'd wandered for days, her mind addled from heat and thirst. She told me it wasn't fair that Daryl had died, it didn't make sense. He'd had a future to look forward to.

"My son worked so hard, and now he's gone," she said, reaching for me, straightening my tie. "Tell me about Daryl. Tell me about my son."

I could have told her any number of stories about Daryl. I could have told her about the time in fourth grade when I brought my GI Joes to school, and Roger Buchanan called me a pussy for playing with dolls, so Daryl hit him in the face with a rock. Or I could have told her about all the times me and Daryl sneaked into the fields behind his house to play Marines, and how we'd annihilate entire enemy armies, just the two of us, and when some imaginary militant tossed an imaginary grenade, Daryl was always the first jump on it, to give his life for me. But I didn't tell his mom any of those things. I didn't know how to say them. When I opened my mouth, nothing came out but dry air.

Daryl's mom asked me to come to her home and meet the out-of-state relatives. I made some excuse, apologized and left. I wanted to travel as far and fast as I could from that sad little town, but as soon as I turned onto the main road, I felt too weak to drive. I pulled into the first restaurant I came across, not because I was hungry but because I needed somewhere to sit and think. It was a shit-hole restaurant, and none of the pictures on the menu looked appetizing, all gray and greasy.

I didn't give a damn about food. All I could think about was Daryl, who would never be a pilot because we'd buried him underground. And how his mother wanted me to say something nice about her son, but I'd failed. I felt like my whole life had been that way. I'd wanted so much, but wanting didn't make it real.

At this point in time, it had only been a few years since I'd stopped believing in God. I could still remember how comforting it felt to trust that everything happened according to his will, to believe that even if I couldn't make sense of his complex logic, all things— somehow—worked out for the best. And maybe, despite all appearances, there was a god. Maybe there were two: the god of life and the god of the muddy hole where we buried my friend. Everybody spends so much time dreaming, but the only sure thing is there's a hole waiting for us, someday, sooner than we know.

Light from the windows pushed impotently against the shadows of the diner. I made up my mind to order, snapped the menu closed and looked around for a waitress. There she stood, studying me from the doorway to the kitchen. Unmistakably Carmen—holding a pot of coffee like a sidearm. Unmistakably older—a thin streak of gray winding through her deep-black hair. Unmistakably pregnant—her dirty apron unable to hide the bulge beneath.

Our eyes locked. It was as if an invisible cord connected us. It had always existed, only it had grown long and loose from our years apart. Now its elasticity returned, dragging us together, drawn tight by the weight of Daryl's corpse.

I saw her.

She saw me.

And I knew, and she knew.

Smoking and Other Bad Decisions

I didn't have any cigarettes, so I called you, and you came over with cigarettes. We smoked on the deck out back. The wood glistened from last night's rain and smelled subtly of rot. Pretty soon everything smelled like cigarettes. You told me about your grandfather, how he kept forgetting his name and trying to break out of the nursing home. You said you always mean to visit him but somehow never do. You held up a cigarette and watched it degenerate into ash and smoke. You said you'd been thinking about switching to ultra-lights. You said maybe it was time to cut back, maybe take up jogging or yoga. That's rubbish. I want to live a short life with you and smoke cigarettes.

FAWN

Monday again. Melinda watched the road like a fourth-grader eyeing a page of long division. Inevitably, some jerk in an Escalade cut her off. She thought about honking the horn. She thought about raising her arm to give him the finger. She wondered why some people do things and travel and live with fierce intensity, and the rest of us wake up to the 6 a.m. alarm and a long drive to work.

That's when she saw it.

A deer grazed on the far side of a field bordering the highway. Melinda, suddenly oblivious to traffic, swerved onto the shoulder. Gravel crunched under her tires as they rolled to a stop. She exited the car, crept to the passenger side and leaned against it. She stared at the animal. If it sensed her presence, it gave no sign. The deer nonchalantly munched grass near a small patch of woods barely thirty yards away. It was young and bore no antlers, so she could not tell for sure if it was a buck or a doe, but in her heart, she knew it was a doe.

* * *

Melinda had a thing for deer. They reminded her of the best years of her life, when she was young and lived on her parents' farm. She remembered waking one morning to a deer peering at her from right outside her window. She clutched her bed sheet to her chest, frozen, staring into the animal's eyes. All of nature seemed to exist in them. They spoke to her of sun and trees and rivers and endless fields of grass. The eyes seemed to say that life was beautiful, and it was the randomness, the dangerousness, of life that made it so. Melinda blinked. In the time it took for her eyes to flick closed and open again the animal disappeared.

For many weeks afterward, Melinda had experienced a recurring dream in which she was a deer. She ate flower petals and raced through deep woods, nimbly dodging between the trees with a gait more like flying than running. She felt strange when she awoke, as if she had lost something. The dream came every night at first. Later it returned sporadically, once every few weeks. Then months passed between its visits, then years.

* * *

Melinda stood by the roadside, heedless of cars whizzing past. She stayed there even after realizing she was late for her shift at the warehouse. She watched the deer until it wandered into the woods. The sun hung high overhead. Sweat beaded on the back of her neck. By now her boss would be rabid. She surprised herself by not caring.

Melinda spent the next ten hours inspecting packages in a medical warehouse. She took her usual spot by the conveyor belt. Clear-plastic breathing masks, flexible tubes, intravenous therapy bags, cold-metal heart sensors—her job was to keep an accurate accounting of such things. She made small marks on a clipboard as inventory moved down the line. The conveyor belt was loud and never stopped rolling. During the seventh hour of her shift she looked at her clipboard and imagined the marks were the days of her life, imagined the conveyor belt carrying those days away from her, ferrying them deep into the warehouse until some stranger dumped them into a box, closed the flaps, taped them shut.

On the drive home, she peered out the window when she passed the field where she'd seen the deer, but night had fallen and she saw nothing. At the house, her husband had eaten dinner without her. She warmed some leftover Rice-A-Roni in the microwave and ate alone at a long kitchen table. The rice was cold in the center, but she ate it anyway. Later she sat in the living room. It was dark except for the TV, which cast weird light over her husband and the rest of the furniture. He sat in a recliner and listlessly flipped channels before settling on some black-and-white war movie.

"All I want to do anymore is sleep," Melinda said.

If her husband heard her, he gave no sign. She wandered upstairs to the bedroom. Hours later her husband joined her, lying fully clothed with his back to hers, a foot of space between them. If Melinda had been awake, she might have asked herself a series of difficult questions.

Is this the life I wanted?

Do I still love him?

Was I born for something more?

But Melinda was already asleep. She dozed peacefully, dreaming of a new but familiar life. Dawn broke in the deep woods. The morning air burned cold in her lungs and smelled of damp soil and pine. She stamped the forest floor with a cloven hoof. She licked dew from leaves of ivy. Melinda darted through the trees with a gait more like flying than running.

Skipping School

Joanne told her teacher she believed in God. Her Bible class teacher. It seemed like the safest possible answer. Afterward, she fidgeted in her seat, her hand automatically reaching down to smooth the pleats of her skirt. Joanne hadn't expected the question, hadn't expected anything like it. Mr. Galloway's class was usually the most boring hour of her day. He liked to go on and on about King David and the Ten Commandments and Leviticus. Joanne couldn't have cared less.

When the teacher asked the question, Joanne had been staring across the classroom at Brad. Brad was the only boy at school with red hair. She gawked at him not because she had a crush on him or anything like that, but because he wore his orangish mane in a tight crew cut like her brother before they shipped his ass off to Iraq.

"Of course I believe in God," she had answered, her head snapping around to face her teacher, her cheeks flushed because—just maybe—she'd been caught ogling Brad.

"Why?"

Joanne struggled with the question. What did he mean? One didn't need a reason to believe in God. It was automatic, something she had done all her life. She believed because her mom and dad had raised her to believe. And because all the priests at church expected her to. Because her parents had dragged her out of bed for Mass every Sunday for all her twelve years, and what was the point if he wasn't real? And she believed because her grade in Bible class pretty much depended on it. When she couldn't answer the question, Mr. Galloway turned it over to the rest of the class.

"Because the Bible says so."

"Because *someone* must have created the universe."

"Because he talks to me when I pray."

"Because without him there would be nothing."

They sounded like good enough reasons to Joanne. She wondered why she hadn't been able to think of any. She watched her classmates—boys in their starched-white shirts, girls in their plaid skirts and tube socks—work themselves into a near-panic raising their hands, squirming, vying to show off their smarts. Joanne didn't feel like she belonged. Soon enough the lecture changed course. Mr. Galloway told the story of Job. Joanne zoned out. She'd heard it a thousand times. She glanced across the room at Brad.

Later in the hallway, Joanne marched toward math class while Amanda tagged along behind her. Amanda tried to tell her what it felt like to kiss Stephen from down the street. Normally Joanne would have been extremely interested in any story about kissing Stephen, but just then she was preoccupied by math class. The doorway loomed before her. It would be division today. Long division.

"Let's ditch, Amanda, just you and me," Joanne said, turning suddenly and gripping her friend by the wrist. "Let's skip class and go to the park, the mall—anywhere. Let's get out of here."

Amanda looked at her like she'd suggested shooting Father Mattias in the face. Joanne sweetened the deal. She had a little money left over from her birthday. They could buy McDonalds. And then there were the cigarettes. Joanne had been pilfering them from her mother for weeks, one or two at a time. This morning she'd meticulously wrapped them in a red bandanna and shoved the package to the bottom of her purse next to a letter from her brother.

Joanne could see from the expression on her friend's face that she very much wanted to smoke these cigarettes. But inevitably she chickened out. Sometimes Amanda was a real cunt.

* * *

Joanne sat by herself on a park bench. She munched a cheeseburger and sipped Coke through a straw. The afternoon was colder than she'd expected, and she cursed herself for leaving her coat on the rack in homeroom. She'd thought about retrieving it but didn't want to risk drawing attention to herself.

She had expected the park to be full of kids. The park was lousy with them on weekends. Now that she thought about it, it made perfect sense that they'd be in school, but regardless, the park felt weird without them. She looked at the empty swings and considered playing on them but decided against it. The thought of swinging by herself in the park depressed her.

Her cup gurgled as she sucked out the last of the soda. It didn't even taste like soda anymore. It tasted like watered-down shit. She put the empty cup and her cheeseburger wrapper on a heap of garbage overflowing from the trash can beside the bench. Then she fished through her purse for the cigarettes. She took out one cigarette, a lighter and the letter from her brother. She struggled with the lighter. She hated those things, hated the way the teeth on the metal wheel dug into her thumb, hated how it would slip and she'd lose the flame at the last possible instant. Eventually she got the job done. She held the flame to the tip and breathed in until it caught. She exhaled. Joanne didn't particularly enjoy smoking but understood it was what one did while ditching school. She took another puff. She wondered what all the fuss was about.

The letter sat on her lap. It wasn't going away. She'd made her brother promise to write her every week, and now he'd been gone for six months and this was the first she'd heard from him. The day the letter arrived in the mailbox she'd considered throwing it the fuck away. Now she had folded and unfolded it so many times she feared the seams wouldn't hold and it would fall apart into rectangles.

She opened it and read it again. Her brother began by calling her that nickname he knew she hated. Then he said he was very, very safe and having as good a time as possible, considering the circumstances. He said the food was mostly normal, but he'd tried some Iraqi cuisine and it was weird, goat and lamb prepared in the strangest way possible. He said sometimes he felt like joining the Army had been the right thing to do, and other times he just didn't see the point, like the war was useless and he had given up what should have been the best years of his life. He asked her to be good to mom and dad. He told her to "buckle down" in school. He told her he loved her. Joanne remembered he'd said the same thing the day he left, and it had been the first time she'd heard those words from him.

She folded the letter closed for what must have been the thousandth time. Her cigarette was spent. The sun was setting. She walked through the park and across the street to the sidewalk that would take her home. She approached a pawn shop at the corner by the crosswalk. A newscast played on a big television in the window, and while the news typically bored her, this segment was about the war. Soldiers mobilized in the desert. Lots of them. She couldn't hear the anchor but could tell by his demeanor something big was happening.

Joanne noticed her own reflection in the glass. She always hated her hair, a helmet of frizz—not quite blonde, not quite brown. Her hair was a car wreck. An afternoon at the park had not improved it.

A man crossed the street. He stopped a few feet from her and watched the television through the window. He rubbed his jaw and sighed.

"What a mess," he said, turning to walk away.

"What's going on?" Joanne asked. "What's happening with the war?"

"Huh?" the man said, acting like he hadn't understood her even though Joanne knew goddamn well he had.

"The war," she said, pointing to the television. "Is something going on?"

"Oh yeah, yeah," he said. "Marines are going somewhere. Fallujah or somewhere."

"So it's just the Marines?"

"No, no. It's everybody. Tanks, planes—everybody. What a mess."

The man rubbed his jaw again and left. Joanne watched the television for a while. Eventually she turned around and leaned against the shop window, glancing at cars whizzing past as the sky turned dark. She folded her arms against the cold. Then she fished through her purse for another cigarette. She pulled out a crooked one with a small ball of lint clinging to the filter. Joanne straightened the cigarette and removed the lint. She lit it on her first try.

Joanne thought about the war.

She thought about her brother.

Joanne made up her mind about a few things. She was already late and knew her parents would be frantic, so she decided to go home as soon as she finished the cigarette, or maybe after another. She felt cold, but the smoking warmed her. Joanne decided she no longer believed in God.

THERMITE

After the shooting, I heard a ragged voice beyond the hill call out in Arabic or Urdu. Black smoke stung my eyes and smelled of thermite. I didn't understand the words but knew they meant it hurt so much to die.

The Worst Chinese Restaurant in Detroit

The bitch at table three growled something nasty because I didn't refill her Coke. I recognized her. She came in last week. Stiffed me on the tip even though I treated her nice as apple-fucking-pie. The bitch shook her glass impatiently. I smoothed a hair out of my face and disappeared into the kitchen.

Ryan reached into the meatbag and pulled out a handful of frozen beef chips for the skillet. Most of our ingredients came off a Sysco truck on Tuesdays. All but the meatbag. Only Mr. Wong knew the origin of the meatbag.

"Need more meat," Ryan said.

"Use some broccoli," Mr. Wong said. He owned the place. He treated the staff like dogs but in front of customers was all charm, like a jolly Chinese saint. He'd be like, "You want Mongol beef? Is good, yes? Is *very* good."

Mr. Wong was Puerto Rican and spoke perfect English with a Midwest accent. Nobody in the kitchen called him Mr. Wong. We called him General Tojo.

I grabbed a relatively clean plate and covered it with gray rice and a scoop of yesterday's moo shu pork from a vat beneath a heat lamp. I poked it in the center.

"This is cold," I said.

"Bullshit," Ryan said.

He grabbed the plate and stuck it in the microwave for forty-five seconds. I took the steaming mess and a big smile to table five.

Out in the dining room, the bitch at table three tried to flag me down, called out "excuse me, Miss?" but by then I was already taking another order. Sweet and sour chicken, which we didn't serve, but if I brought him a plate of General Tso's he probably wouldn't know the difference.

I avoided table three on the way back to the kitchen. A small victory, but I couldn't go on winning forever. Sooner or later I'd refill her goddamned Coke because pissing her off wasn't worth losing a lousy three-dollar-an-hour job. Not with my landlord breathing down my neck. The bitch at table three owned me same as everybody owned me.

Ryan wasn't in the kitchen, so I gave the order to one of the Asian girls. She nodded but didn't say anything. The Asians never spoke or looked at me. They were right off the boat, probably some indentured servitude bullshit. I didn't know anything about it and hoped to keep it that way.

I found Ryan out the backdoor smoking a joint.

"My turn," I said, snatching it from his fingers. I took a long drag, held the smoke in my lungs until they felt ready to pop.

"There's more where that came from," he said. "Come over after work."

Ryan smiled at my tits with his serial-killer grin. He stood at the tail end of a long line of people trying to own me. He wanted to ram me with his diseased cock, in my cunt and ass and mouth. I smoked his joint and said nothing.

Ryan went inside to check on the General Tso's. I stayed out and finished the roach. I leaned against the brick wall, looked at the city. Beyond all the blight and post-industrial bullshit, I saw the skyscrapers downtown, the GM building and the rest. They looked chrome and crystal, rising to pierce the heavens, beautiful and perfect and far away. They might as well have stood on the surface of Mars, because they weren't built for people like me. Sometimes I think the people who work in those towers are a different species, some new kind of human armed with diplomas from private colleges, beautiful people who sip Ketel One vodka martinis at fashionable bars while discussing character arcs from programs on HBO.

After a minute or two I found myself back in the dining room delivering another plate of meat parts and sugar sauce. I noticed General Tojo talking to the bitch at table three.

"Cuntfucker," I said, all quiet-like under my breath.

"We so sorry," he said in his fake pidgin English. "So very, *very* sorry." He looked like he might commit seppuku right there in the dining room. Instead he snapped at me.

"You! You go! Get Coke cola!"

I lowered my eyes and tried to look abashed. I knew the game well enough to play along. Because when somebody owns you—like the bitch did, like General Tojo did—you do what they tell you. You refill their fucking Coke. It's the proper order of things. So I served her a fresh one. Smiled big. Apologized cloyingly. Bowed my head as if to a queen.

Maybe I spit in it and maybe I didn't.

ALOHA STATE

Jillian opened her eyes on the beach. A Hawaiian beach. A strange beach of black volcanic sand. Her first—she hoped—of many exotic beaches. She reflected on how a mere fifteen hours earlier she had boarded a plane at the international airport in Huntsville, Alabama. As she looked around the beach, she felt that her situation in life had improved radically.

They'll never drag me back to Alabama.

Jillian had a habit of mentally cataloging people in either of two categories: *Beyoncé* or *Billy Ray*. The uniformly tanned, bikini-clad denizens of the beach belonged, clearly, in the *Beyoncé* category. The majority of her friends and family back home in Mobile, however, dwelled in the other. Jillian watched a well-muscled Hawaiian man wade into the cove up to his chest, then take off swimming, sunlight gleaming on his tan skin.

Another Beyoncé.

The more she looked at all the beautiful people, the more she became aware of her own whiteness. She was the whitest person on the beach.

"I'm a zombie," she said to her sometimes-friend, Britney. "The living dead."

"Don't wear so much sunscreen," Britney said. "You'll never tan like that."

Jillian was not surprised that her friend would give her such a terrible piece of advice. When Britney and Jillian had been classmates at McGill-Toolen Catholic High School in Mobile, Brittney had consistently earned her spot in the *Billy Ray* category. That is, until she'd graduated and enrolled in the University of Hawaii at Hilo. Although it pained Jillian to admit it, Brittney was now a probationary *Beyoncé*.

Jillian noticed, and not for the first time, that although she was skinnier in most places than Britney, her friend lacked the small roll of fat around the waist that Jillian had become so adept at hiding. Jillian also thought Britney looked too small for her breasts. She sighed. Her sometimes-friend was clearly winning.

"Is there some law in Hawaii that everybody has to wear a bikini?" Jillian said.

Britney leaned toward her, spoke low and conspiratorially.

"Everybody wears them," she said. "Even the fat girls. Even when they're pregnant. And *all* the Hawaiian girls are pregnant. They're lucky to make it out of junior high before getting knocked up."

Jillian subtracted a few *Beyoncé* points on account of Brittney's racism. She'd hoped to leave that shit behind her in Alabama. Hawaii didn't strike her as fertile ground for racism. The island was too pleasant, the weather too mild, the people—by all appearances—too happy. Jillian looked around at the sand and water. Kids floated on neon inflatable rafts alongside their parents in the shallows of a blue cove. Snorkelers bobbed around several large triangles of black stone. Behind the beach and stretching out to sea stood an ancient wall of lava. A group of guys climbed it and jumped off at the highest point, splashing into the water, laughing and scrambling back up the ledge. Across the bay, a shelf of green land sloped to the sea, and farther still the island rose to become a mountain, Mauna Kea, its snow-capped peak visible among white ropes of clouds.

"I want to do something fun," Jillian said. "I want to go snorkeling."

"Don't waste your time with that," Britney said. "It's boring. Trust me. Boring."

"I want to see a turtle," Jillian said.

"We'll go out to a club tonight," Britney said. "I know a place. Very classy. Not too *Hawaiian*, if you know what I mean."

Jillian mentally subtracted another point. She yawned and stretched and noticed a Hawaiian guy with a tribal pattern of tattoos on his shoulders and arms. He reclined in the sand and looked in their direction. Because of his sunglasses she couldn't tell if he was looking at her or Britney or someone behind them.

"I'll take you to Hapuna this week," Britney said. "It's gorgeous. You'll die. White sand and everything. Not like this shit." She scooped a handful of black sand and let the coarse grains sift through her fingers. "You should see the sand on Oahu. It's like baby powder. Bay-bee powder."

"Ok," Jillian said, still looking at the man across the beach.

Jillian lay down and lowered her sunglasses over her eyes. A grove of willows dropped long needles onto the sand. She looked at the sky and branches overhead. The needles grew in triangular patterns and whipped in the breeze. Britney called out to a friend and told Jillian she'd be right back. Jillian heard the sound of flip-flops slapping against sand. Seconds later, the well-tanned guy with the tattoos plopped down on Britney's towel. He held a joint between two fingers. He told Jillian his name was Kana'i. He pronounced the second syllable like "nah" and the last like "ee." He offered the joint to her. Jillian considered flashing her *get lost creep* look, but instead she introduced herself and accepted the joint. She swept her eyes over his chest, board shorts and legs. He told her the water was "fierce" today.

Jillian immediately classified Kana'i as a male *Beyoncé*. She asked him if he surfed. He laughed and said yes. He said it was easy and he could show her. He waved his hand at the beach. He said the scenery here was nice but the surfing was shit.

"I surf Honoli'i," he said. "Honoli'i is better."

"Mr. Kana'i, you should take me to Honoli'i." She inhaled and held the smoke in her lungs.

"Anytime," he said. He took back the joint. Smoked.

"Now?"

"No," he said, coughing. "Tomorrow. In the morning. I love to surf in the morning—when I'm the only guy on the water, and I know later it will be crowded, but maybe for half an hour the whole ocean belongs to me."

Jillian advanced Kana'i to the very pinnacle of her *Beyoncé* category. If he didn't stop talking about waves and the ocean soon, she would have to create a new and better category, something just for him and the rest of the gods.

"Surfing sounds nice," she said.

"It is."

"I'm impressed you wake up so early in the morning."

Kana'i laughed. He took another drag off the joint.

"I don't do much in the mornings," she said.

"Your loss."

"If, by some tragic coincidence, I wake up before noon, all I do is eat cereal."

Kana'i told her she needed to find her passion, and after that, everything would fall into place. Jillian sidled up to him. They shared the joint for a few more minutes until Britney returned. She gave Kana'i a particular look. It was not a nice look. She turned to Jillian, arched an eyebrow. Kana'i offered her the joint, but she waved it away. Britney told Jillian it was time to leave.

"I'll stay," Jillian said.

"How will you get home?"

"I'll take her," Kana'i said.

"Mr. Kana'i will take me," Jillian said.

Britney packed up her belongings. After she left, Kana'i and Jillian scooched closer together. Jillian felt that Kana'i was a person she could open up to. She told him all about college and majoring in sociology.

She said she loved her classes but didn't know what to do with her life. He, in turn, explained the maintenance work he did for the county. He said a job is a job, and his wasn't important to him, not as important as surfing.

"I don't have a career," he said. "I have a lifestyle."

Kana'i smoked and looked around. He pointed to the crescent-shaped apartment tower rising above the trees behind the beach.

"That's where I live," he said.

* * *

Sooner than she expected, Jillian found herself standing on the balcony of Kana'i's apartment. She put her hands on the metal railing. It was painted blue, and in places the paint had chipped away. Outside she saw more willow trees, and tiny people lying on the beach or swimming, and dark blue patches of water in some places and light blue in others, and how the wind rippled the surface. Towering waves exploded against the lava rocks guarding the cove, and even from on high Jillian heard the roar, saw tiny drops of spray glittering in sunlight.

"The crazy thing is how fast you start taking it for granted," Kana'i said. "You'll be like, 'well, it's another beautiful day. What's on Netflix?'"

He placed his hand on the slenderest part of her waist, slipped a finger underneath the elastic of her bikini. They faced each other and kissed, and he reached behind her to unfasten her top. She felt the ties loosen, his hand suddenly on her breast. He motioned toward the bedroom. She stood pale and naked in the colorful light of late afternoon. She followed him inside, climbed into bed, kissed him again, lay on her back. He fucked hard at first but ran out of breath— much sooner than she would have expected of someone who spent so much of his life on a surfboard. They rolled over to put her on top. She looked at his face but didn't like the shapes his mouth made. She noticed the surf posters covering the wall behind his bed. Jillian looked at images of women in better shape than herself. She closed her eyes to focus. She arched her back, tried to move her hips fluidly like rolling waves. She thrust out her chest to make the most of her tits. She wanted him to see all of her, to know her. She wanted to pretend this was more than it seemed—spiritual—like he would never forget her, as if their lives would be forever changed.

Afterward he lay on his stomach, his face turned away from her. She touched his back—softer than she expected—and traced his tattoos with her fingers. On the beach he'd appeared quite muscular, but now she thought he looked a little pudgy. Some of what she'd mistaken for muscle—she realized—was fat. He wasn't unattractive. He just wasn't who she'd believed he was.

Another Billy Ray.

Jillian imagined how it would feel to be his girlfriend. To eat with him at restaurants and watch TV together on the couch and always have sex with him until the end. Usually when she had sex with a boy he became her boyfriend. Usually.

"Do you want to go surfing or something?" she said.

"Not now," he said.

He opened a drawer on his nightstand, took out rolling papers and a sandwich bag of weed. He smoothed a spot on the bed and rolled a joint.

"I want to see turtles," she said. "People said there'd be turtles in Hawaii."

"You haole girls are all the same," he said. "All you haole girls love turtles."

"Girls are stupid," she said.

He laughed. He covered his mouth with his hand and wheezed like an old man.

"Turtles," he said, shaking his head "It's just funny. The way you people lose your minds over them. It's hilarious."

"What's wrong with turtles?"

"Nothing. I love turtles." He grinned and showed off a mouthful of yellow teeth. "Turtle soup, turtle meat, turtle tacos. What's not to love?"

Jillian considered what he'd said. She realized that, in the course of her life, she had found herself in many similar situations—situations she'd hoped to have left behind in Alabama. She had allowed herself to believe that coming to a new place would be different, the people would be better. Somehow she always had trouble with people.

In a corner by the closet she noticed a snorkel and mask. She walked across the room and picked them off the floor. She asked Kana'i if she could borrow them.

"Sure," he said, licking the joint to seal it. "I never use them anymore. Snorkeling sucks. You just float around and look at fish."

"I mean, can I borrow them right now?"

"Getting late," he said. "I don't have time to teach you."

"I know how," she said. "I've done it before."

Once when I was seven.

He looked at the snorkel and mask. He looked at her. He looked at the joint.

"Do whatever," he said.

* * *

The beach was nearly deserted by the time Jillian returned to it. The water felt so unexpectedly cold she considered going back to Kana'i's apartment and bugging him for a ride to Britney's. The sun had disappeared behind a thick bank of clouds, changing the color of the water from blue to dull gray. In the distance, a lone surfer floated on his board. She walked deeper into the water, stumbling along a rocky path. When the water reached her breasts, she put on the mask and snorkel. She took a few practice breaths before plunging her head

80

beneath the surface. The water was clearer than she'd expected. A white fish swam figure eights a few inches from her foot. Jillian kicked off from the sandy bottom and floated. She saw another fish, wide and yellow, and a bloom of coral folded like the creases of a brain.

"This is some crazy shit," she half-said, half-hummed through the snorkel.

She swam above the reef, looking down to see bullet-shaped fish painted like modern art. She saw an angelfish with a streamer trailing off its top fin. She hoped she wasn't bothering them. She turned and swam somewhere deeper, then she surfaced and tread water. She looked to the shore, with its willow trees and dark sand. She found the spot on the beach where earlier she'd sunned herself with Britney. The memory of it didn't feel real. Her entire life seemed foggy, like a dream.

The sun slipped behind the mountain. In the early-evening dimness, the ocean took on a darker shade of gray. Jillian swam toward the beach. She could only see a foot or two in front of her through the darkening water. She heard a splash. A large, strange thing appeared in the murk. Massive. Green or gray. Scales and claws. She jerked her head out of the water and kicked away to avoid colliding. She breathed hard through the tube. After a few seconds and with great trepidation she peeked underwater again.

The turtle was easily more than a yard long, with a knobby shell and a face beaked and scaly like a dragon's. The turtle pivoted with quick strokes of its webbed feet. Jillian and the reptile looked at each other. She imagined she could transmit psychic messages through the water and into its brain.

"Hello, Mr. Turtle," she transmitted.

Even with her head submerged, she heard surf crashing faintly on far-off rocks.

"Tell me, Mr. Turtle, are you really alive? Am I?"

The turtle flexed its jaw.

You are not a girl, she imagined it saying. *You are not white.*

"Mr. Turtle, you are being silly."

I have swum these oceans for a thousand years.

"I don't know what I'm doing anymore. I don't know why I'm here." Jillian paddled with her hands to stay afloat. The air from her lungs roared, a little, through the snorkel.

Don't go back to the beach.

"But I have to. I have to go back or I'll drown."

Follow me.

The turtle turned toward darker water.

I will show you what it means to live.

Follow me, child.

Follow me into the sea.

LAYOFF

Bert delivered the bad news after lunch. He handed everyone on day shift a pink slip of paper informing them that they'd be laid off from the factory. They were not fired, not exactly, the paper assured them. They could be recalled at any time.

"What's this all about?" Daniel demanded of Bert.

"Just read the paper," Bert said, scratching his stomach.

"I read the damn paper," Daniel said. "I want to know what this is all about."

"I feel like shit, you know I do," Bert said, still scratching. "Look at the bright side. At least you're not fired."

Daniel's shift didn't end until the evening, but he went home immediately after his conversation with Bert. He did not punch out at the time clock.

"What the hell's the point?" he muttered as he slammed shut his car door and gunned the engine. He hated the job. The boredom. The mind-numbing tedium. But he needed the paychecks.

* * *

Hours later he sat on the couch in his apartment, TV remote in hand, flipping from news network to news network. None of them said anything worth hearing. Now that he'd lost his job, he no longer felt the news applied to his life. Already he felt disconnected.

His wife Betty was surprised to see him when she arrived from her job at the restaurant. She walked in on him watching TV in the dark. In her greasy apron, she smelled of cigarettes and red meat.

"The factory laid us off. All of us, the whole shift," he said before she could ask. It was easier to talk about if he dragged his coworkers into it.

"What will we do?" Betty said, her face ashen, her eyes huge. "How will we make rent?"

"Relax," Daniel said. "I'll find something new in no time."

And that's how it went all night, with Betty in a mild panic and Daniel gently consoling her, reasoning with her. He told her they would be fine. They'd tighten their belts, stop eating out so much, maybe cancel cable TV until things turned around. They would be fine, he said, just fine.

The next day at breakfast, he read the help wanted ads in the newspaper classifieds. Then he drove all over town to fill out applications. He submitted paperwork at the unemployment office. He felt like he wrote his name, address and phone number at least a thousand times. Back at home, he washed the dishes and swept the kitchen. He didn't want Betty to think he was lazy.

That's how he spent his days of unemployment. He'd bust his ass all afternoon to fill out applications at any place in need of labor, then come home and clean up. Betty acted fine at first. Supportive, even, for a while. But as the days turned to weeks, she became increasingly distant, irritable. She wouldn't let him touch her at night. She didn't say much, but when she did, she lost her temper. She accused him of not doing enough around the house. He'd made a good start, she said, but he did less and less every day. This was true, he admitted, but he was her husband, after all, not her butler. And he'd had a run of bad luck, and couldn't she cut him some slack?

One morning, instead of going out to put in applications, he sat at his computer and searched for jobs online. Then he spent the afternoon watching TV. The next day he skipped the computer and just watched TV. And he would have done the same the next day except he felt like if he spent another second in the apartment, he would lose his goddamned mind.

It occurred to him that the apartment complex had a pool. He had never used it, never had time. Now, time was all he had.

* * *

At midday during the week the pool was nearly empty. Some kids splashed around in the shallow end, their parents nowhere to be found. Daniel dove into the deep end. The water felt cold, but he acclimated quickly. He hadn't gone swimming in years, not since he was a child. He had forgotten how much he enjoyed it. Best of all he liked swimming underwater. It was like flying, only in slow motion. He could fly for as long as he held his breath.

Later, exhausted, he floated on his back. Waves rocked him gently. Chlorine stung his eyes, but it didn't bother him much. Under the midday sun, the water looked impossibly blue, the poolside stark white. Overhead the contrail of a plane split the sky into hemispheres. Daniel floated between the water and August sunlight. He felt like he was living at the end of time.

It wasn't long before the blonde in the stars-and-stripes bikini showed up. She carried an inflatable raft under her arm. It was mostly blown up but not all the way. She kicked off her flip-flops, sat poolside with her long legs in the water and inflated it.

Daniel watched her from the deep end. He leaned back against the poolside, his arms outstretched on sun-warmed concrete, supporting his weight in the water. He watched her blow into a small plastic nozzle. He swam laps back and forth across the deep end, hoping he cut a fine figure.

The girl put the raft in the water and climbed aboard. She started in the shallow end, but momentum carried her to deeper waters. Daniel swam some more, but as she came close, he stopped and rested again on the side of the pool.

"I hope I'm not in your way," the girl said from behind a large pair of sunglasses.

"You're fine," Daniel said, out of breath from swimming.

"If I'm in your way just tell me," she said.

"Don't worry about it," he said. "I'll swim underneath you."

"Will you?" she asked, and even from behind the sunglasses he saw her arch an eyebrow. She told him she was working on her tan

"I never tan. I can't," he said. He felt her eyes sweep over him, over his chest, ghost-white from days spent beneath the factory roof.

"You just need to work on it," she said. "Come back tomorrow. Spend an hour or two out here every day. You'll get your tan. Anyone can do it. You'll see."

They talked awhile longer. He learned her name was Tanya and she attended college, a marketing major. She was recently single after leaving a relationship that should have ended in high school. When he told her he was laid off from work, she appeared quite sympathetic—more so, he noted, than anyone else he'd confided in. He mentioned that he was married. She nodded and seemed disinterested. She didn't ask about his wife.

He swam some more laps after that, diving underneath when she floated across his path. And wherever the raft carried her, he was aware of her eyes on him.

* * *

That night at dinner, he stifled the urge to tell his wife about Tanya. She was all he wanted to talk about, all he could think of. But he knew better than to mention her.

"Laundry's piling up in the hallway," his wife said, sighing.

"I'll get to it tomorrow," he said.

"Did you put in any applications today?"

"Sure," he lied. "Plenty."

* * *

He spent the next day at the pool. He hadn't been there long before Tanya showed up, lugging her raft. He waved, and when she stepped into the water he swam over, challenged her to a race. Daniel and Tanya spent the day together, waging splash fights, practicing handstands on the bottom of the pool, playing in the sun and water like neither of them had since they were children.

* * *

At dinner, his wife remarked on his tan. Daniel admitted he'd spent some time at the pool.

"Must be nice," she said.

"Losing a job is no picnic," he said through a mouthful of meatloaf.

"Oh, I don't know. It sounds OK to me. I wait tables all day. You hang out at the pool. You watch TV. It sounds pretty goddamned OK to me."

"It's not like that," he said.

"Did you apply anywhere today?"

"Look, I've applied all over the city. I've been everywhere. Something's bound to turn up. It just takes time, is all."

"I thought you said you'd take care of the laundry."

"Tomorrow," he said. "I'll do the laundry tomorrow."

* * *

The sun was shining when he arrived at the pool. Tanya was already there, floating on her raft. Quietly, he slipped into the water and swam to her beneath the surface, holding his breath until he burst out and dunked her. She squealed as she went under, then resurfaced in a tangle of wet hair.

"You bitch," she said, laughing and gasping for air. She slugged his shoulder. "I'll get you for that."

87

She lunged at him, and he dove out of the way, took off swimming. When at last Daniel allowed himself to be caught, the contact of her skin thrilled him as she pulled him down.

They played in the pool for hours, stopping only when they became exhausted. They floated in the sun, she on her raft, he on his back.

"What do you want from life?" he asked, staring up at the empty sky.

"What do you mean?"

"Why are you majoring in marketing? What do you want to do?"

"I don't know," she said. "I don't care. I just want a job that pays decent. Something that isn't miserable, you know?"

"I know."

She rolled off the raft, her thin body making hardly a splash. She swam to him. They regarded each other, face to face. A wet lock of hair curled down her forehead. Her green eyes appeared to glow.

"Let's race," she said.

He reached for her, placed a hand on the curve of her back, tugged her close. The kiss was electric and made Daniel feel something leap inside his chest. Her lips moved in time with his as they tread water, their legs churning through the cool, blue expanse.

Tanya pulled away.

"I should go," she said, swimming for the ladder.

"I'm sorry." Daniel paddled slowly behind her. He clung to the ladder after she'd climbed out, all strength fled from his body.

Tanya toweled herself dry, then walked back to the edge of the pool. She towered over him, cloaked him in her shadow.

"I'm so sorry," he said.

"Don't be."

She knelt by the ladder and kissed him quickly and lightly on his lips. She stood up. She fished her raft out of the pool and walked away.

"Will I see you tomorrow?" he called out to her.

"Take a wild guess."

* * *

That night in the apartment, he could hardly sit still. He swallowed dinner without tasting it. He flipped TV channels haphazardly, didn't take anything in.

"You forgot to wash the clothes today," Betty said, arms folded, sitting away from him in the recliner in the corner.

"Fuck," he said. "I'm sorry."

"You're always sorry," she said. "You don't work. You don't help around the house. I can't take much more of you being sorry."

"We already had this argument."

"Then get a job."

"I'm trying," he said.

"Try harder. Take a job at a gas station, a grocery store, a fast-food place. Do something. Do anything."

"I can't live like that."

"Well I can't live like this," she said, standing up and storming out, maneuvering around piles of unwashed laundry in the hallway before slamming the bedroom door behind her.

Daniel slept on the couch that night. Before falling asleep, he considered doing the laundry, then he just didn't. He dreamed about his old job at the factory—the gray walls, noise from the conveyor belt, boredom, hypnotic repetition. In the morning, he awoke to the sound of his wife getting ready for work. After she left, he fell asleep again. A few hours later the phone rang. He answered it, groggily, while lying on the couch. Immediately he recognized Bert's voice.

"Good news, boy-o," Bert said. "The layoff is over."

89

Daniel sat up.

"What do you mean?"

"I mean you're going back to work. The factory took an order, a big one. Everybody's being recalled."

"That ... that's great," Daniel said.

"I need you back on Monday," Bert said. "Can I count on you?"

"Sure," Daniel said. "I guess ... I mean ... sure. Sure, you can count on me."

Daniel hung up the phone. He sat on the couch for a time, staring at nothing. The news would make Betty happy, of course. It had been hard, recently, between them. The news would make it easier. Daniel thought about the factory, about the long gray walls. He lay down again and tried to sleep. He did not go back to the pool.

The Loneliness of the Retail Banker

The thing to do after cheating is *shut up about it.* You've probably been quite circumspect up until now, arranging meet-ups and phone calls in secret, generating covert Facebook accounts with passwords etched so deeply into your psyche you'll never have to write them down. And you expect something small like that will give you away, something physical you've forgotten—a receipt scrunched in your back pocket, a tube of unfamiliar lipstick, dinner purchased on the wrong credit card, her panties kicked under the sheets at the foot of the bed. That's how it would happen in a Lifetime movie (trust me, I've seen them all), but more than likely your wife will find out when somebody tells her.

It might be her friend Vanessa who heard it from someone at the bank. Or one of your own friends could spontaneously grow a conscience. Maybe you'll tell her yourself. Because you'll feel sorry, so awfully sorry, and telling her is the only way to exorcise the guilt. Or maybe one night when you're driving home from Vanessa's party your wife will lay into you for ignoring her all evening, and you'll listen and keep listening until you snap and tell her everything. "I fucked her," you'll say. "What do you think about that? I fucked her and liked it."

The thing to do after cheating is *put it behind you.* Remind yourself that you are fundamentally the same person you were before the infidelity. Redouble your efforts to make your marriage work. Because it's a good marriage. Or it was. It was good on your honeymoon, when the two of you sipped pineapple and rum on the patio of the largest hotel room you had ever seen, and a salt breeze blew in from the Bermuda coast, and for some reason you were captivated by the way her red hair swayed as she laughed, and you looked at her and told her you'd never been so happy, and you didn't just say it to be romantic. You meant it. You were happy.

The thing to do after cheating is *remember how to have fun again*. Powerful forces—inertia, global capitalism, the Lifetime Movie Network—have conspired against you. But you can beat them. You can turn off the TV and look into her eyes. You can talk about ideas, if you still have any. You can spend time with your wife. Take her camping. Maybe she'll go. You can sleep with her under a dome of stars.

The thing to do after cheating is *change your life*. Quit pushing credit cards at the bank, where you spend hours instant messaging the secretary upstairs and fantasizing about fucking her in the vault on a pile of other people's money. Wave goodbye to your coworkers who hate their lives just as much as you do but are afraid to leave because the economy sucks, and what else would they do? What would they do? Flip off your boss, the pale one with the spots on his forehead that look like cancer. On your way out the door, grab him and kiss him right on the cancer spots. You're free now. You're on your way to a new life, one marked by noble poverty and adventure.

But you won't. You won't dare. Here's what you will do: you'll stay shackled to your cubicle where, day after godforsaken day, you'll input consumer information into databases while knowing full well that the bank's interest in all this is to mire poor people in additional debt. Your hard work will earn a promotion for cancer-face. You'll go home to your wife who is equally exhausted from her own soul-sucking employment. You'll spend hours ignoring each other. You'll prepare separate dinners in the microwave and eat them on opposite ends of the couch while watching Lifetime movies. When you can't take it anymore, you'll retreat upstairs to Facebook and a dark room. You'll jack off to a photo of the secretary, or what she represents—a new life, a better one, with passion and intensity and sex.

Sooner or later you'll spill your guts in the car after Vanessa's party. And there will be silence. And muffled sobs. Enjoy it, because later comes the screaming. And amid the worst you will notice how her green eyes, which usually are glassy from television, have come alive with a fire you haven't seen in ages, and you'll watch her hair sway as she hurls ugly words at you—while digging through the closet, throwing things into suitcases—and you'll remember how it always sways like that, and you'll want to laugh but can't, the scene is awful and you can't, and she'll say "I'm going to mother's," and you'll say "Your mother is a cunt," and it will all be over but the lawyers.

You will feel fine at first. You'll look forward to fucking the secretary and all the free time you can spend doing ... something. Time will pass. You'll make certain adjustments. Eventually you will find yourself awake after midnight, and you will drink but not be drunk— not drunk enough—and you will play your Xbox in your underwear. Beside you will be a half-eaten bowl of Cheerios. You will catch your reflection in the warm milk. You will wonder why you are crying. The thing to do after cheating is to learn to be alone.

You Are Not Eighteen Anymore

The 6 a.m. alarm ruined everything. It rang and rang and murdered Spencer's very satisfying dream about the intern. He opened his eyes, groaning as the fantasy evaporated. The dream had been a good one, so real, almost like a memory. Anyway it ended too soon.

He began his day on the treadmill—twenty minutes of jogging with hand weights to work his arms. Then, winded, he completed three sets of sit-ups and push-ups. He did all this for the intern. Once upon a time he'd been naturally thin. But those days were over. The gradual slowing of his metabolism had provided an unpleasant twist in the story of his life. Now he tended to hover a few pounds above his target weight. That's why, for breakfast, Spencer munched on a handful of baby carrots. Washed them down with water. He finished the meal with a multivitamin from the cabinet above the stove. Among all the granola and protein powders, he noticed a candy bar in a glossy wrapper. He'd bought it after work one night but then chided himself and hadn't eaten it. Hadn't thrown it away, either. Now that he saw it again, his mouth began to water. The candy bar looked much better than carrots. Spencer closed the cabinet. He rooted around the fridge for more cold vegetables. He had to look good for the intern.

He thought about her on the drive to work. She was pretty and young. Smart, too, and much more advanced than he had been at her age, which was eighteen. In a week she would leave for her first year at college. Something about her reminded him of every girl he'd ever dated. He wanted to feel again what he had felt for them, wanted to fill his empty places with her heat, wanted back again everything he had lost. He would ask her out. It would be easy. She would say yes.

Probably she would say yes. He turned up the radio and accelerated, felt the thrum of music and pistons. He would ask her out.

When he arrived at the office, the intern—her name was Ashley—sat at the desk beside his. Dark hair, dark skin—she had a certain way of cradling her chin in her hands, and sometimes while speaking she swiveled her chair compulsively back and forth. She did this for him and no one else. He took it as a good sign.

"You look nice today," he said.

"I look nice every day," she said. "I like your T-shirt."

The shirt featured a silk-screened image of the Trix cereal rabbit. In a cartoon bubble, the rabbit said, "Trix are for kids!" Every other guy at the office wore a tie and jacket. Spencer usually wore a tie and jacket.

A pile of unfinished ad copy sat on his desk. He took the first sheet off the stack, pretended to scrutinize it. Mostly he thought about Ashley. Later he asked her if she'd finished reading *The Curious Case of Benjamin Button*. The university she would attend in the fall had already assigned an intimidating reading list. He enjoyed talking to her about books. None of his friends cared about books anymore. They had all wanted to be artists and writers when they were young but grew up to program computers.

"It was ... I don't know ... weird or something," she said. "A lot different from the movie."

"Brad Pitt," Spencer said. "Sex machine."

Ashley shrugged. "Maybe like ten years ago," she said.

"It's a great story," Spencer said. "I love it. It's all about aging and death—how sooner or later everything good in your life turns to shit."

Ashley put her hand on his shoulder.

"And you wonder why I don't like it."

For the rest of the day, Spencer attempted to concentrate on his job. His work had never seemed so pointless and boring. He would begin to read the reports stacked on his desk, and then his mind would just drift away. He would sigh sometimes and look at Ashley.

At the end of the shift, she surprised him by asking his age.

"Thirty."

"Get out."

"I'm old," he said, sucking in his stomach. "Seriously. But nobody believes it. Everybody thinks I'm twenty-four."

"Maybe it's your clothes," she said.

Spencer changed the subject. He talked about movies. He asked her if she'd seen the horror film *Drag Me to Hell*. He described it as a throwback to Sam Raimi's early films, classics like *Evil Dead* and *Army of Darkness*. This new one was a lot like the movies he'd made years ago, only more refined and mature.

"It's like you're speaking a foreign language," she said.

And suddenly he felt the moment had arrived—this was it, what he'd been building toward all summer. All he had to do now was ask her out to the movie. She wanted to be asked, expected it. He was not too old for her. He was not delusional. The words—the question—formed in his brain. He lost them somewhere on the way to his lips.

* * *

Spencer was not in the best of moods when he returned to his apartment, alone. The space had never seemed so quiet. He called himself names: coward, loser, creep. He wasn't sure they were true names but knew he had to say them. They made him feel a certain way, like he'd been cut open with a knife, and even while the wound hurt it felt good, a little, too.

He looked at the treadmill in the corner, at his worn running shoes. He owed himself three solid miles.

"Fuck it," he said. He went to the cupboard for the candy bar.

He ate it on the couch. He'd meant to turn on the TV but then just didn't. He stared at a blank wall, hardly took any notice of it. The wrapper crinkled pleasantly as he tore it open. The chocolate tasted as sweet as he remembered, maybe sweeter. The caramel melted in his mouth.

Spencer wanted to die.

This was not the happy ending he'd expected. It was not even a proper climax. This was shit. It was all shit.

His imagination ran wild. He'd been so close, had been on the verge of steering his life in a happy new direction. Somehow he'd blown it. The intern would leave for college soon. No eighteen-year-old would ever want him again. He'd fucked up his very last chance.

Or had he?

He reached into his pocket for his phone.

Ashley picked up on the third ring, recognized his voice. She sounded surprised and excited all at once.

"A movie? Tonight?" she said. "I'd love to."

He arrived at her parents' house at sunset. She answered the door, yelled to her mom and dad that she'd be back late. Then she was his. She wore blue jeans and a tight shirt revealing the barest hint of midriff. Nothing fancy. Merely perfect. For a moment they stood facing each other on the porch. He took her hand to kiss it and somehow ended up with his lips pressed to hers. She felt softer than he expected, her kisses sloppy from lack of experience. He held her, noticing she fit him perfectly, as if some divine sculptor had gravened her just for him. He kissed her youth, her energy, her spirit. He kissed the illusion her life would be easy, her choices simple.

* * *

The crinkle of the candy bar wrapper lured Spencer back to reality. He blinked. He stared at the phone, its face still empty and black. He stared again at the blank wall. He heaved a sigh, eventually, and looked at the bar—nougat and peanuts torn by his teeth, made mushy by saliva. It didn't look like much. He took a bite. A mouthful. Chocolate and creamy caramel. Sugar. The candy bar tasted delicious.

The story of his youth had been a good one. He'd written chapters full of romance and adventure—the kind of story in which a person might lose himself, a long and meandering tale of character arcs and climaxes, enough to create the illusion that the plot would continue advancing without end. Only it did end, as stories always do.

Now the tale was told.

Now the book was closed.

Kandahar

I swallowed a pink pill after breakfast, gripped the sink and stared at my face in the mirror, waited for waves of happiness to overtake me, for my gray world to explode into rainbows and zebras and hippy flowers. It didn't work. Sometimes drugs aren't enough.

Later I smoothed my tie and locked the apartment door behind me. I set off down the hallway thinking dark thoughts. Mostly I dwelt on my job and all the ways my boss would make my life suck for the next eight hours. This line of thinking metastasized into a generalized anxiety, Terrible ideas ran like a hellish news chiron through my brain—the president is incompetent ... possibly a madman ... the banks are collapsing ... the economy is fucked ... jobs are fucked ... the Middle East is at war ... the war is all our fault ... partially all our fault ... our fault and the fault of our incompetent president ... possibly a madman.

I froze mid-step. Blinked. Rushed back down the hall to make sure I'd locked the door.

Once I finally made it outside, I saw Lucid Thomas sitting on the stoop. He didn't live in the building, but it was his favorite stoop. He muttered at everybody who walked by. A lot of people walked by. As I came down the steps, he stood up to ask for a dollar, but when he saw it was me, he nodded and sat down.

"Do you know what a water buffalo looks like after it's been shot?" Lucid Thomas only had five or six stories. They were all about Vietnam, and he told them over and over. "It looks dead." Lucid Thomas used his hands to form an animal shape in the air. "It looks dead."

"I know all about it," I said. "Tell me something new."

Lucid Thomas thought for a moment.

"Dolphins are psychic," he said. "If you swim up close, they'll read your mind."

"I don't think that's true," I said.

"Do you know what a dolphin looks like after it's been shot?" he said.

I walked away, headed up Broadway to the metro station. I passed red-brick buildings and people and an occasional tree. I concentrated on the trees, hoping they would grant me the peace that modern pharmacology had failed to make good on.

My friend Jeremy died. According to Facebook, he died. I found out last night. I didn't think I'd sleep but then did, a little, I guess toward dawn. Jeremy died in Afghanistan, and I don't know any details yet, and maybe I never will.

I remember something Jeremy said when he was on leave during his first deployment. This was several years ago, when he served in Iraq. He said that after we got through with Fallujah, it looked just the same as those black-and-white photos of places like Dresden and Yokohama that got bombed in World War II. Craters in the streets. Buildings dark and gutted. He told me I wouldn't believe it even if I'd seen it. He said he'd seen it and still didn't believe it.

I walked along the sidewalk and looked up at all the buildings, imagined them burning until they were nothing but skeletons, the ghosts of buildings. I wondered what would happen to all the people who lived in them. The crowd thickened as I approached the station. It perched high above the street, with a long covered stairway leading up to it. It looked like some giant mechanical insect looming above the neighborhood. I stood at the foot of the stairs. Commuters jostled past me. I thought about my job—the abject grayness of my cubicle, the long hours I would spend there, the pointlessness of it all, the bleakness, the way the sickly light projected by my computer monitor would bathe my face, painting it with a corpse-like pallor.

"Fuck it," I said. Not that anybody cared.

I took a tentative step backward. To either side, people streamed up the stairs, heading to work or school or wherever else they were required to be. I turned and walked away from the station. With every step, I grew more confident in my decision. I kept going for a long time and wandered without any clear direction. Eventually I ended up at Sakura Park. I sat on the concrete steps of the gazebo and looked at the cherry trees. Tiny petals dropped off limbs and fluttered for a second before joining others in a pink mat on the ground. Kids played on swings and a slide. I tried to remember what it felt like to be like them, to forget everything bad in life and run around wild and happy. I remembered when me and Jeremy were kids and played in parks, played army and war. I remembered shooting him with a stick that was a gun and how he fell in the grass. He played a trick on me and pretended to be dead. I crept up as he lay motionless and peaceful. "Wake up," I said, nudging him. "Wake up." His eyes popped open blazing blue and we took off running.

I sat and listened to kids and birds and the soft noise of wind shushing through the cherry trees. I pretended to be happy. When that didn't work, I stood up and started walking again. I went to this Mexican restaurant where I'd eaten with Jeremy for the last time. It was only about a year ago. This time, the waitress tried to put me in some crappy booth in the back. I stopped her and asked for a table by the window. The restaurant was sort of depressing, the kind of place that feels greasy no matter how many times they wipe down your table. Sitting alone in the back would have made me want to kill myself.

I remembered how, when Jeremy was here, he'd ordered the enchiladas. I stared at the empty seat where he should have been sitting. I remembered how he was always so skinny in high school, but the last time I saw him his arms had grown thick and hard. The army turned him into a different kind of person, one with skull tattoos and a thin blond beard, like one of the G.I. Joes we played with when we were kids.

I imagined Jeremy sitting across from me in the restaurant.

"So how did you die?" I pretended to ask.

He rubbed his beard and looked out the window at all the people, but he didn't see the people.

"Same shit, different day," he said, peering through time and space. "We were in Kandahar. Everybody was in Kandahar. It was morning and already hot. The lieutenant drove my team in a Humvee through acres of grapevines south of Alkozai village. We'd taken the same road a thousand times. The truck kicked up dust, and with the sunlight and dust and grapevines, we could have been in France. That's what I was thinking about when the shooting started—how maybe once I got out of the service I'd take a trip to see Burgundy or Bordeaux. This next part sounds crazy, but it's true. At first, I thought it was the vines shooting at us—the plants—you know? Like the bullets were just exploding out of the grapes. I raised my rifle and opened my mouth to yell for the team to return fire, but no words came out because there was a bullet in my brain. I saw the sun and dust and bright trails of tracers, and already I was dead. I'd never been so dead in my life."

"What did you say?"

A waitress walked by carrying a tray of dirty glasses.

"Nothing," I said. "Sorry. It was nothing."

I walked around the city for the rest of the day. I swallowed several pink pills, more than the warning label recommended. I wandered through some shops, visited more parks. Nobody in the city cared about Jeremy. Nobody in the city cared about anything. I'd watched them all day. They hailed cabs. Bought donuts and coffee. Listened to music through earbuds. Tapped fingers on their iPhones. Nobody cared. I wanted to stand on a corner and shout, tell everybody that Jeremy was my friend, and now he was dead, and everything was wrong, and everybody should know it, everybody should care. But instead I just roamed the sidewalks for a long time, looking and thinking but never once saying or doing much of anything, because, to tell you the truth, I'm just as useless as everybody else.

I walked back to my apartment in the dark. Lucid Thomas sat on the front steps and grinned as I approached, his teeth yellow like pus from a wound.

"One time I shot a mother and child. Thought they were tigers. Shot 'em in the head."

"I know," I said. "You told me already. You told me a thousand times."

"Kid," he said, incisors flashing like fangs in the streetlight. "I've seen things you wouldn't believe."

I ignored his insanity, which felt familiar and downright cuddly next to the frantic apathy of the city. I climbed the stairs to my rented home. I lay in bed. I tried to watch something funny on TV, but all I could think about were AK-47s and Hellfire missiles. The hour grew late. I closed my eyes and saw Jeremy as I'd known him when we were children. I laughed and chased him through an empty field. I shot him with a stick that was a gun and watched him fall. I crept up to him and saw he was full grown. Sunlight reflected off grass and his yellow beard. His eyes were closed. "Wake up," I said. "Wake up."

MUSIC ROW

I

Trish always sang the best words. I sprawled out on the carpet, looked up at her on the couch as she fingered a guitar. I imagined her words as physical things, objects I could catch as they fell from her lips. I would keep them, squirrel them away somewhere secret.

A lock of hair, wavy and blonde, divided her elfin face into hemispheres as she bobbed her head to the beat. Inwardly I pretended she'd written the song for me. It was becoming a hobby, these lies of mine. They were the kind of lies worth telling. This much is true: I fucked Trish once, a few years ago. Another truth: she considered it a mistake. To her, I was a friend and roommate—nothing more. I tried not to dwell on my failures with her, tried not to overanalyze my love or obsession or whatever it was. I'd lived with it for so many years it no longer needed a name. *It is what it is*, I told myself. I didn't need some stupid word.

From up high on the couch, Trish sang with a country lilt. It's what the city demanded, but she was capable of so much more. She could bend the words to pop or rock or anything else. Trish had a talent for giving people what they wanted. She told the most beautiful lies.

2

Trish left in the morning, went out early to practice with the band or hang out with friends or whatever. It was none of my business. I tried to steer clear of her private life. Anyway I had my own problems. I needed a job. I'd graduated from college in the spring, and as summer gave way to fall, I'd blown through my savings.

I spent the day browsing job websites on my laptop. I churned out stacks of my résumé and mailed them to every newspaper and magazine in the city, hoping to land a job in my field—as a reporter or editorial assistant or something, anything. I needed a paycheck, but I also wanted a job with a little glamour to it. Something to impress Trish. I wanted so much to deserve her.

A mug of coffee cooled on the kitchen table. I stared out the window at all the gainfully employed people commuting along Wedgewood to work. I wondered, idly, how much income they earned and if they found their work fulfilling. I tried not to hate them.

3

That night I went out to watch Trish's band play downtown at The Stage. For at least a week I'd seen her face staring at me from flyers posted all over the city. At the show, old guys with beards tapped their boots on the wooden floor. Young dudes in tight T-shirts whistled and stared at Trish's tits. Everybody loved her. It occurred to me that she might have a future in music, after all. Maybe it wasn't the pipe dream she'd always thought it was. Which would be great. Just fantastic, really. Except her relative success only served to amplify my failure. Every day, I fell a little further from deserving her.

I bought a longneck at the bar. I remember this part clearly because it cost me eight bucks. And then I turned and sort of weaved my way through the crowd toward the stage, careful not to bump anyone or spill my beer on account of the eight bucks.

Trish stood in the spotlight, wailing on her guitar, creating a sound that transported me to another world, one where I didn't have to worry about finding a job because I'd always have a home with her. Trish sang of dreams coming true, innocence rewarded, love that lasts for all time. It was bullshit and the crowd ate it up.

Then she started in on the solo, only for some reason that night it wasn't a solo, and the bass player, Trent, sang along with her, sharing a microphone, and their lips moved close enough to kiss, and as they exhausted the final note they stared deeply, longingly into each other's eyes, and I saw everything I needed to see.

I left the club. I would've dumped the beer on the sidewalk except it was the last one I'd be able to afford in the foreseeable future. I nursed it while leaning against a brick wall outside. Up above I saw the tops of skyscrapers from a few blocks away. They gleamed like something out of a sci-fi movie. I couldn't imagine ever working in one of them, couldn't imagine stepping inside and casually punching a number in the elevator. It would be like entering another world. I sipped my beer and knew it would never happen for me.

The streets were packed with tourists looking for a good time. Policemen on horseback patrolled the crowd. Custom cars with neon undercarriages and spinning rims prowled the avenues. Streetlights painted everything yellow. The air felt good, the temperature mild. I stood outside for a while before returning to the club.

After the show Trish bought me another eight-dollar beer. She invited me to come along with the band to the Mercy Lounge for more drinks. I declined, made up some lie about being exhausted. If I saw Trent, I probably would have punched him in the face.

I waited until after she left before walking home. I couldn't afford a cab, and I didn't want her to know how broke I was. The streets downtown were packed, but the crowds thinned out long before I got to our apartment. I walked blocks and blocks, and when I arrived what I wanted more than anything else was to fall into a beer-induced coma. Instead, I powered up my laptop and polished my résumé.

4

Sometime after 3 a.m., Trish came home, smiling and happy and singing and drunk. She asked me—commanded, actually—to have a beer with her. Without waiting for an answer, she opened the fridge and pulled out two Yazoo IPAs. I saved my résumé and shut my laptop.

Seeing her like this reminded me of the night she fucked me sophomore year. This was long before she'd become a semi-successful country singer and I had failed at life. Back then we were just students—me at the big public university south of town and her at Belmont with all the rich bastards. Back then I deserved her, or half-way deserved, or at least I believed I did. It really felt like a gut-punch when, after our night together, we woke up and got breakfast, and we were joking around about everything, and all the sudden her voice became quieter and more serious, and she told me she didn't regret what happened, not exactly, but she didn't want to repeat it. I told her I understood, promised everything was cool and I wouldn't make any drama. And then, naturally, for the rest of that year I dedicated myself to making her mine. I was relentless. I pushed and pushed. Eventually some of our friends intervened, took me aside and told me to back off, that I was only hurting Trish and hurting myself. So I backed off. Way the fuck off. Made myself scarce around the apartment for a while. Put some distance between us. Sometimes I wondered if she missed all the attention.

Trish fumbled with the bottle opener. I took it from her. Tiny puffs of fog escaped after I popped off the caps.

"I want to feel like this forever," she said after her first swig.

"Like what?"

"Like I'm flying. Like I'm goddamn Wonder Woman. Like my life will only get better and happier."

"Right," I said after a while. "That's how I feel too."

We drank. She sang, swaying and bobbing her perfect head. It wasn't long before her eyelids drooped. I led her by her the hand— small and perfectly formed, with fingernails that had never been chewed—to her room, leaving her unfinished beer on the table. I maneuvered her into bed, and she rolled over to make room for me. I climbed in beside her. She sang. I worked up the nerve to put my arm around her. Before dropping off to sleep I whispered, "I want to feel like this forever."

5

I got out of bed in the morning before Trish woke. I opened my laptop and emailed my résumé to every Podunk newspaper within fifty miles of the city. These were places where I'd be embarrassed to work, but I was beyond desperate.

Trish got up around noon. She investigated the cupboard before offering to buy me some pancakes at IHOP. And after breakfast we drove to Centennial Park. It was a weekday, but I was unemployed, and Trish didn't have band practice. We were free people.

On the way to the park we stopped at the Mapco Express on West End to buy a loaf of bread for the ducks. I noticed a help-wanted sign in the window. The store looked kind of skanky, but it didn't seem like the kind of place where people got murdered.

Me and Trish walked around the duck pond at the park, throwing bits of bread to the birds. They went crazy, fighting, honking, flapping for every scrap. We walked side by side. I pointed at the weirdest ducks and she laughed. Everybody who saw us probably thought she was my girlfriend. We bummed around the park all afternoon. At sunset we sat on the big stone steps of the Parthenon. It was built several decades ago to look like the one in Athens. The one in Nashville wasn't the real thing. It was just another beautiful lie. Trish sat Indian style and told me how a talent scout from a record company was coming to one of her shows. This wouldn't be for another month.

"You'll come, won't you?" she said. "I need you to clap the loudest."

"Like I've got anything better to do."

Trish laughed and punched my shoulder.

"I bet you've got a secret life," she said. "I bet you're a spy for the CIA. I bet every time I turn around you're assassinating somebody."

From where we sat on the steps, I could see all the way across West End. I saw the neon lights at P.F. Chang's. I wanted to eat there but couldn't afford it.

"I'm just a guy without a job. A guy who can't catch a break. That's all I am."

"Things will get better," she said, smiling the smile that was making her famous. The setting sun turned the sky to magma. I hoped she'd lie to me forever.

6

Travis was my manager at the Mapco Express. I put in an application once my bank account and self-esteem bottomed out. Travis hired me. He told me he didn't see too many college graduates at the Mapco Express. Travis wore his mullet spiked. Tattoos of skulls, dice and naked women danced the hoochie-coochie down his arms. His unbuttoned work polo framed a manly tuft of chest hair.

"People come to the gas station for many reasons," Travis said to me on my first day. "Mostly they come for gas. Also, for beer and cigarettes."

Travis was a wise man. I followed him around the store. He showed me how to rotate the hot dogs, break down the slushy machine and mop up vomit. Finally, he took me on a tour of the beer cooler. The beer cooler was important. It was dark and cavernous, and it was the source of the store's greatest profits. And it was haunted. Travis told me all about the Colonel, the Confederate ghost who dwelt there. I asked Travis why a Confederate ghost would haunt a gas station beer cooler.

"Because that's where the beer is," Travis said.

Travis told me the Colonel's story, how he'd ridden home after peace was signed at Appomattox. He rode fast, anticipating the nights he'd spend with his young wife whom he'd left alone at the plantation. But when he arrived, he walked in on his wife buck naked with a Union deserter. A goddamned Union deserter. This did not sit well with the Colonel. He shot them both where he found them, in his marriage bed. Then he pressed the pistol to his own temple and blew his brains out.

"The Colonel did not deal well with disappointment," Travis said.

Travis used to play in a rock band. Travis played drums. His band did shows all over Nashville, at places like the Exit/In and the Cannery. But then his bandmates knocked up their respective girlfriends. After that they found real jobs, because they didn't want to raise their children on Ramen Noodles and peanut butter sandwiches.

"I was going to be the next Eddie Van Halen," Travis said, reaching his hand out to the sky.

By now my shift had ended. Travis lent me a cigarette, and we smoked behind the store.

"Life," he said. "Life is full of shit."

Travis was an OK boss.

7

After two weeks I picked up my first paycheck. It wasn't much, but it paid for a night out with Trish. We headed downtown, shared the sidewalks with the tourists and local kids looking to get wasted. We ate steaks at Demos. We took a walk by the river. It smelled like trash but looked beautiful beneath the stars. We drank beer at Paradise Park and fancy vodka cocktails at McFadden's. She made me dance with her at the Wildhorse Saloon. I danced terribly, but Trish was too drunk to notice. Later we watched some girl take the stage at a club in Printers' Alley.

"You're much better than her," I said.

She told me I was full of shit. She smiled big with her white teeth. Trish wanted to be the best at everything, still believed such a thing was possible.

Neon lights painted the sidewalks red and blue. Some guy came up to us at a crosswalk, told me he needed money for a ticket out of town. I lied and told him I was broke. Me and Trish crossed before the light changed because no one was coming anyway.

At a small table on the sidewalk, a black woman thumbed a deck of tarot cards. Trish paid fifteen dollars for her fortune. The cards said someday she'd be famous, a big star like Reba McEntire or Taylor Swift. The lady asked me if I wanted my fortune told. I said no, even after Trish offered to pay. My future was the last thing I wanted to know. The night had been good. I didn't want to ruin it.

8

I had to work at the Mapco Express on the night Trish played for the talent scout. Travis told me my shift was non-negotiable. At first, I was frustrated to miss her big show, but the more I thought about it, the more I felt just goddamned peachy. I had no doubt she'd perform admirably, impress the socks off everybody and make all the men in the room fall in love with her. Trish had the words, and the words would make her famous. And as I labored through the early-morning hours to stock the display cooler with beer, I'd had just about enough of Trish's success. I felt like I was losing touch with the part of me that could feel happy for other people. I felt less and less each day I spent working the cash register for the drug addicts, con artists and Vanderbilt snobs who frequented the store. Every shift at the Mapco took a chainsaw to my sense of empathy.

I could see the future. Years from now, Trish would pass me on the street, recognize me—barely—as a relic from another lifetime. We would make awkward conversation for approximately forty-five seconds. We would not quite know how to act. She would walk away and out of my life forever.

I hefted a six-pack of Rolling Rock and loaded it into its assigned row in the display cooler. As I withdrew my hand, I scraped a finger against the jagged edge of a bottle cap. I cussed and sucked blood from the wound. I stood alone in the dark cooler. At the periphery of my vision I almost thought I caught a glimpse of the Colonel, staring at me from the corner with his pale, dead eyes. I looked again but there was nothing. Maybe I'd seen a flicker of light from the cooler's fluorescent bulb or a fog of condensation from the air vent. There was a lot of beer to stack before daylight. I got back to work and tried not to bleed all over the inventory.

That was my life. Stocking beer. Selling cigarettes. Making change for a dollar. I'd never expected to bottom out so soon. Every day I sank further into shit—up to my knees, my cock, my neck. I couldn't breathe anymore because my whole life had turned to shit.

"Goddamn it," I said, alone in the cold. "Just God-fucking-damn it."

Somewhere beyond time and space, I'm certain the Colonel nodded in genteel agreement.

9

I had the next night off work. Trish took me out to Jackson's in Hillsboro Village. The Village is probably the best place in Nashville. It's got the Belcourt Theater where I once watched Casablanca at midnight, and Boscos restaurant where they brew their own beer, and Book Man Book Woman, a used bookstore that's probably too good for Nashville, a town that celebrates words only when they're sung by someone beautiful.

As soon as we got a table and some drinks, Trish shared her good news. The talent scout loved the show. A record deal was imminent—the company would pay them to cut the tracks, the CD would be sold in actual stores, Trish was about to see a payday like never before.

"This is it," she said. "This is what I've worked for. Worked my ass off."

Trish slung back her head, swallowed a shot of tequila. A warm breeze blew ripples through her hair. I caught her green eyes and hoped she'd never look away.

"This is my chance," she said.

"You deserve it."

"Shit," she said. "Nobody deserves nothing."

The sky was clear and the streets, packed. It was Friday. Everybody wanted to get as drunk as me and Trish.

"Deserving is just a word," she said, slurring her speech a little. "Just something people made up to make sense out of chaos. A word to draw meaning from meaninglessness."

"Nobody deserves shit," I said.

I looked across the street. I saw the bankers in their sharp suits, college kids out on dates, women with Prada handbags, and a black man crouched in an alley, begging for change.

"Charles Barkley drives a fleet of Hummers, while special-ed teachers eat goddamned peanut butter for dinner," she said. "Nobody deserves nothing. This world we live in, it is what it is, you know? People use such fancy words—honor, justice, altruism, sin. They don't mean anything. They're just words."

"What about love?"

Trish laughed. Our waiter came over. He looked like a punk rock musician. We ordered Jack and Cokes.

"Now that one's tricky," she said, running a slender finger around the rim of an empty shot glass. "Love is a nice idea, and it's easy to sing about. I mean, everyone wants to believe they'll find it, that they'll matter to someone, that they won't die alone. Fuck. It sounds pretty good to me. I don't know if it's real. I mean it's not. Probably it's not. But I want it to be real—you know? I want to believe in love."

That's when I took Trish's hand. It felt so small in mine, her bones fragile, hollow like a bird's.

"I love you," I said. "I always have. I love you every day. I love you right now."

Trish looked down at the table, at the ground beneath it strewn with discarded plastic forks and used napkins.

"Please not again."

Trish suffered beautifully. Somehow I tore my eyes off her. I looked back across the street at the homeless man. His plaid shirt was dirty and thin, like he'd been wearing it all season.

"No one will ever feel what I feel for you," I said.

Trish just kept staring at the ground.

The black man reached out his hand to a passing woman. She wore a nice yellow dress and her hair done up like she was on her way to meet someone. The black man had a face like tight leather stretched across bone.

"I'm sorry," Trish said. "I'm so sorry."

As the woman passed, she turned to the man. She gave him a piteous smile and nothing more. I was hardly surprised. It's something you see in Nashville all the time. I turned back to Trish, gave her a good, hard look. I considered saying a few things but elected to take the high road and keep my mouth shut. Anything I'd have said would have been nothing but a bunch of words that didn't mean anything, anyway. I was sick of words. I needed something else. I made up my mind to go home and start packing up my stuff and move out. The time had come, time to stop beating my head against the same old wall. Maybe I'd leave Nashville altogether. Maybe I'd find a new city, new friends, some new girl to love. And maybe Trish would miss me once I'd gone. Maybe she'd write a song for me. Something sweet and a little sad. Maybe someday I'd hear it on the radio.

FREE LOVE AND TELEVISION

And there I was, imagining myself on the receiving end of a thorough examination by the entire male cast of Grey's Anatomy, when you started up again—all *holy shit* and *motherfucker*—and I remembered, with great regret, that I was not lying prone on a table at Seattle Grace Hospital but, rather, slouching with you on the couch in our living room, like always. A Gilmore Girls rerun played on TV. You told me you were tired of all my *chick shit*, tired of *Rory* and *Lorelai* every *goddamn* night. You told me I only ever thought about myself. You snatched the remote and changed the channel to some basketball game, even though my episode was only half over, and it was a good one, the one where Rory oversleeps after cramming for a Shakespeare exam and hits a deer on the way to school. Just as you settled back down beside me on the couch, LeBron made a drive for the basket and my phone lit up with a text from this guy at work. Usually I'd blow him off because of his obvious *I just want to fuck* vibe, but against my better judgment I read the text—a single word, *drinks?*—and was all set to ignore him when LeBron dunked the ball—really slammed the fuck out of it—and you stood up yelling *goddamn* again and punched the wall and threw the remote to the floor so hard the batteries popped out. And without thinking much about it I typed *see you in one hour,* and as my thumbs formed the words on the screen I understood I had become a new person—a crueler and better one—and if I could see into my future it would look like a sky full of stars.

Turtles Are Reptiles of the Order Chelonii

Janice was the first. Janice who sat in the cubicle next to mine. Her phone rang just before noon, and she answered it like nothing was wrong. Because as far as she knew—as far as any of us knew—it was a day like any other, and we'd all work our eight hours and punch out and complain to each other about the grind like always. Anyway, the assistant manager was on the line, and he called Janice to his office. After she left, I got back to work and forgot all about it. Ten minutes later, Ray from accounts came over.

"Something's up," he said.

He motioned to Janice's empty chair.

"They took her downstairs," he said.

A phone rang among the nest of cubicles behind me. Bryan answered it. He stood up and walked to the assistant manager's office. Everybody stopped working and looked at him and whispered.

"Motherfucker," I said.

It wasn't long after they took Bryan downstairs that Richard got a phone call. And then Angela and Barry. Nobody in the office was working anymore. We stood around in groups, talked about how Richard was only a year from retirement, so maybe it wasn't so bad for him, but Janice needed the insurance because her daughter had spina bifida, and what would she do? What would she do?

Derrick got the next call. And that one really shook me, because Derrick was solid. If they could get rid of Derrick, nobody was safe.

"Maybe it ends with Derrick," Ray said.

"Six," I said. "A nice, even number."

"Maybe they'll stop at six," Ray said.

That's when my phone rang. Somehow, I convinced myself it wasn't mine, maybe it was somebody else's phone at a cubicle nearby. Then I saw my incoming call light blinking red. I looked at the phone. It rang again. I looked at Ray, the hardness of his face, the tension. The phone rang again. Everybody looked at me. It made me mad how they stared, the pity in their eyes, the poorly veiled relief. The phone rang. I looked back at Ray. He sighed. The phone rang.

* * *

A few hours later, I was sitting on a beach. My briefcase lay on the ground in front of me. The managers had sent for it after taking me downstairs. I wiggled my feet to dig pits in the sand with the tips of my black leather shoes. It wasn't a good day to be at the beach. The sky had clouded over, and the same wind that churned the gray waves blew open my suit jacket and whipped my tie backward. Whenever the wind gusted, I felt the pressure of the tie around my throat.

I don't know how long I sat there. Wave after wave came ashore, turned to foam against the beach. Sometimes the water came close to me, and sometimes it receded, and I knew if I sat there long enough it would get me. If I sat there long enough the tide would come up and wash me away.

The beach was mostly empty, probably on account of the weather and because tourist season had ended a few months back. After I'd been sitting for long time, a girl—she couldn't have been older than twelve or thirteen—walked in front of me down by the water. She stared intently at the sand like she was studying it, then glanced at me for a second before looking down and walking away. A few minutes later she came back and gave me a good, long look.

"Sir?" she said. "Do you know much about turtles, sir?"

"No," I said. "All I know is corporate accounting."

"I'm looking for turtle eggs," she said. And then, as if to reassure me, "It's for school."

118

"Fifteen years," I said. "Sarbanes-Oxley. Quarterly earnings reports." I gestured toward my briefcase between my legs in the sand. "Fifteen years and they wouldn't even let me go back inside, wouldn't let me say goodbye. Like they were afraid I'd make a scene. Like they thought I'd do something crazy."

The girl laughed, which seemed weird to me because I hadn't said anything funny.

"Fifteen years," I said, raising my arms.

The girl laughed again. She sat in the sand behind me. She told me her name was Makayla and she was writing a report on turtles for science class. She said she thought if she could find a turtle egg and bring it to class, her teacher would give her an "A."

Listening to her talk about turtles reminded me of one of those nature documentaries I'd seen awhile back on TV. I told the girl that turtles bury their eggs on the beach, but the lights from all the hotels and condominiums confuse them so that they can't figure out where to make their nests. They end up wandering onto highways and getting hit by trucks.

The girl stood up and looked at the building behind us. Evening had hardly begun, but already a floodlight had switched on, illuminating a brick patio.

"Why can't everybody keep their lights off?" she said.

"Nobody cares," I said. I wiggled a shoe in the sand. "Fifteen years. Nobody cares."

"Somebody should do something. There should be a law or something." She punched one of her fists into her palm. "Somebody should smash those lights with a brick."

I stood up and turned around. I took off my shoes. I hurled one of them at the light, then the other. They both missed, slamming loudly against a plate glass door before flopping to the patio.

The girl looked at me and shook her head.

"They're gonna be mad," she said.

"Fuck it," I said, loosening my tie. "I'm going for a swim."

"It's freezing," she said, shaking her head again.

"Fifteen years," I said.

I slid out of my jacket. Unbuttoned my shirt. Threw it to the ground. I lowered my pants and tripped, a little, stepping out of them. I stood tall and squared my shoulders. I wore only my underwear and a pair of black socks pulled up to my calves.

"Jesus," she said.

I grabbed my briefcase out of the sand. I spun around like one of those shot-put guys at the Olympics. I hurled the case and watched it rise like the line graph of a bull market into the sky. The latch sprung open as it reached its peak, and the briefcase began spitting out white sheets of paper like a contrail as it arced down to the water.

"Fifteen years!" I said, sprinting toward the gray sea. I held out my arms, fists raised, flexing my thin biceps like I was strong, straining so my tendons stretched tight all the way up my neck. I heard the roar of surf. And something else, too. Something deeper. It was me. Roaring. My white feet slapped naked against wet sand. I ran to the ocean and roared like the waves rising up to greet me.

THIS PLACE CAN BE BEAUTIFUL AGAIN

I sat by the river, on a damp log half-buried in mud, and watched how the yellow finger of water wound its way through the city, past gutters and factories and underneath bridges, and it smelled like a shit monster from my nightmares. Whenever I read a poem or whatever about rivers, it's always about the beauty and majesty of nature. I bet those writers never saw a river like this one. It smelled like a shit monster from my nightmares.

I heard footsteps behind me slogging through the muck. Cindy took a seat beside me on the log. She wore her nice leather shoes from school, only they were slick with mud. I felt bad about her shoes. Mine were muddy too, but I didn't feel so bad about them. My shoes didn't make me feel anything. But Cindy—I don't know—I saw how the mud had oozed between her laces, and it made me feel just awful.

"It stinks here," she said.

"I know."

"Why did you come here if it stinks?" she said.

"I don't know," I said. "I guess for the same reason you did."

"Not likely," she said, combing her hair with her fingers. "I just came to see if you were still alive."

I glanced at her when she thought I wasn't looking. I liked how her dark hair trailed down to the center of her back. I wanted to touch it, feel its satin-like softness between my fingers. I picked up a smooth pebble and tossed it sidearm to skip it across the surface of the river— but it just plunked underwater. And right as I tossed it, some huge bird, some seabird with white feathers and a long orange bill, took flight. And it seemed like the two were connected somehow, the rock and the bird. It seemed like one couldn't have existed without the other.

"I'm sorry about what those guys said about you," she said.

"I don't care."

"Nobody believes them," she said. "Everybody thinks they're assholes."

"Right," I said. "Why would I care what a couple of assholes think?"

"I told them to fuck off. After you left, I mean. I told them they were full of shit. I told them they were nothing but a couple of assholes."

"Great," I said, kind of waving my hands as I spoke. "Fan-fucking-tastic. Because that's just what I need, some girl sticking up for me. Because, I mean, because now it's not physically possible for me to look more like a pussy."

Cindy fumbled in her purse for a box of Camel cigarettes and a lighter. She lit one and put it in her mouth and puffed a few times. Then she offered one to me.

"Cigarettes cause cancer," I said.

"I wouldn't even bother to smoke if they couldn't kill me," she said. "Go on. Take it. It'll help with the stink."

I held a cigarette between two fingers as she lit it. I took a drag and felt smoke roll down my throat and into my lungs. Smoking made me feel very mature. I know I'm not supposed to say things like that. I know it's a federal offense or whatever to say anything good about smoking. But that's how it made me feel. Like I was some wise old man on a mountaintop. Like I'd done nothing but contemplate mankind and nature for a thousand years.

"Jesus, I've got mud everywhere," Cindy said, showing me a brown smudge on the palm of her hand. It was the same on her skirt and stockings.

"It'll come out," I said.

"I can't let my mom see me like this. She'll go crazy. She always loses her mind."

I took another puff off the cigarette. It wasn't tobacco I smoked but pure wisdom from the heart of the Earth.

"Everything will be OK forever," I said.

We sat and smoked. A black snake wriggled in the water, too far away to trouble us. I watched Cindy comb her fingers through her hair again, and then she yawned, and her arm seemed to stretch out over the river, and I saw all this while exhaling, saw it through wisps and haze. I looked at her hand hanging limp and empty over so much water. I knew what I had to do. I acted fast, before my analytical brain could take over and make me chicken out. I reached for her hand, held it, ran my thumb over the tips of her small, brown fingers. And that was the moment—that one exactly, when we joined in flesh—that was the moment when everything began.

Today We Are Still Married

We'd wrecked the house again. Lisa promised to help straighten up before the party but bailed at the last minute—not that I blamed her, not that I didn't deserve it. I scrubbed dishes as she emerged from the bedroom. Congealed marinara clung to the plates like a zesty red skin, while half-portions of uneaten fish—the ones we'd never bothered to feed to the garbage disposal—turned to jelly at the bottom of the sink.

"You don't get it," Lisa said. "You are incapable, mentally, of understanding how completely I hate her."

Her was Hillary, an old girlfriend from college. Ancient history, right? But I guess history really does have a way of repeating itself. My wife was angry because I'd invited Hillary to the party. It was for my old college friends, the people who used to be closer to me than my family but, for all the usual reasons, I'd lost touch with over the years. People like Hillary.

Most of these friendships had devolved into the infrequent exchange of Facebook messages, but in Hillary's case, the messages weren't quite so infrequent. And as the party drew close, we were texting at all hours of the day and night. Lisa discovered these messages. Lisa was not pleased by what she read. This led to a series of increasingly hostile questions on her part and feeble excuses on mine. Lisa wanted me to tell Hillary to get lost, but I negotiated, told her I didn't want to create drama, didn't want to make things awkward for the rest of the guys who expected her to be there. I assured her that after the party I'd never speak to Hillary again

"No more Facebook, no more emails, no more anything," I said, washing a plate on autopilot, keeping my voice gentle to avoid setting her off. "This is the end."

Liar.

The truth is I didn't know what I'd do. Maybe I'd stop talking to Hillary, or maybe I'd take it underground. Hushmail accounts, secret Snapchat profiles—a second life of espionage and excitement. Once you take that first step, the rest is easy. I didn't have a plan or a strategy. All I knew for sure was that I wanted to see her again. I didn't even know why I wanted that, couldn't translate the emotion into words. But I did want it. And badly. Wanted it bad enough to fight with my wife, to not back down. And, basically, I'd won. Basically. Hillary was coming to the party. I didn't know what would happen when we saw each other again. I wondered if it would change us, breathe new life into the thing between us that had died.

Lisa retreated to the bedroom. I turned back to the dishes. And vacuumed the carpets, cleaned toothpaste spots off the bathroom mirrors, washed a month's worth of laundry I'd picked off the floors, threw away a library of decomposing newspapers and fitted the guest beds with new sheets. I cleaned and cleaned, but none of my domestic productivity made my wife hate me any less.

❊ ❊ ❊

The guys arrived in the evening. Bill and Danny—he went by Daniel now—came in the rental car they'd picked up at the airport. Kendrick drove in from Cleveland, appearing within ten minutes of the others. It was weird at first. We greeted each other more enthusiastically than necessary, hoping a few easy laughs at the outset would carry the conversation for the rest of the night, would take us back to that easy friendship we'd had once but lost. Lisa came to my rescue, asking them about their jobs and families, simple questions I was too nervous to think of. We huddled around the kitchen table, Danny with his Scotch, Kendrick with his dark beer, and through the cigarette haze they could have been the same young men I'd lived with during the best years of my life.

The doorbell rang.

Hillary.

I let the other guys answer it. I sat at the kitchen table with my wife, held her hand, noticed how small she looked, how dark and pretty. We listened, stone faced, to the salutations from the foyer.

"How are you?"

"You look great!"

"It's been forever."

Lisa's hand tightened around mine.

That's when Hillary stepped into the kitchen and obliterated the decade-long gulf that had yawned between us. She was the same girl I'd known in college, and she was someone else, someone older, sophisticated. One thing that hadn't changed was her hair, still dangerously blonde, making Lisa appear smaller and darker by comparison.

Danny mixed a drink for Hillary, and we continued from where we'd left off, talking about the old days. I couldn't stop looking at her, couldn't stop remembering. Seeing her again made me think about what we'd had, and why I'd thrown it away, the flimsiness of my reasoning. I hadn't wanted to be tied down, didn't want to think about the future. All I'd wanted was the freedom to fuck whomever I wanted. Some things never change.

At the table, Lisa told a story about something funny from a TV show. The punch line had a long setup, which she repeated in excruciating detail. But none of us really understood the joke, so when she got to the end we laughed only out of nervous politeness. Hillary shot me a glance. She rolled her eyes toward my wife, silently mouthed, "What the hell?" I smiled like the Mona Lisa.

Suddenly Lisa scooted her chair back from the table.

"Excuse me I don't feel well," she said, bolting from the kitchen.

After a moment I followed her. I found her in the bathroom, knees on the cold tile, hunched over the toilet. Her body heaved. She tried to puke but nothing came out. I sat on the floor beside her, ran my hand down her back. We stayed there awhile, saying nothing. Later she rinsed her mouth at the sink and then climbed into bed. When I lay down beside her, she told me to go back to the party.

"I don't want to leave you like this," I said.

"It's OK. I mean it. It's OK," she said, eyelids drooping. "You haven't seen them in forever. Have a good time. I trust you."

Back in the kitchen, Daniel talked about movies. I took a seat at the table and listened, just sat back and enjoyed their voices. I remembered how Daniel used to keep me up at night talking about directors like Quentin Tarantino and Kevin Smith. Now he dropped names like Godard and Truffaut.

What I recall about that night is the way we insisted on talking about nothing. We hadn't seen each other in forever, but instead of sharing much of anything personal we discussed sports and music and YouTube videos. We kept at it for hours, talking and drinking. I'd look around the room and see them, and seeing them made me happy. Then I'd look at Hillary. She'd look back at me and smile like we shared a secret, something unspoken between us. Something the long years had failed to kill.

Eventually I saw Kendrick yawn, and then I yawned, and I told my friends it was time for me to turn in. I shook hands with all the guys, showed them to their rooms, made plans to go out for breakfast in the morning.

* * *

I found Hillary outside on the deck. Alone. I joined her, careful to shut the sliding glass door behind me. We leaned against the railing, maybe a foot of space between us. The moon had set, so it must be starlight I remember reflected in the lake's choppy surface. The wind felt cold, but I didn't mind.

"Getting late," I said, for no particular reason.

"So here we are," she said. "You wouldn't believe how I've missed you."

She moved close. I felt the soft pressure of her chest against mine. This was it. This was the moment we'd been building toward. Every email we'd exchanged had taken us here. Her voice on the phone last week, all the times I'd jacked off to her memory—the whole trajectory of our lives had carried us irrevocably to this place, to this lake beneath these stars.

It would be easy, I thought, the simplest thing in the world. I looked at her, and the more I looked the easier it became. A decision had to be made. In my mind I walked a tightrope. I could have fallen in one of two ways, and then I did fall, and not for any reason. I didn't have a game plan or rationale or motivation. I just fell.

"This can't happen," I said.

She kissed my neck with lips too soft to be real. I smelled her hair, and it made me remember. Her hair smelled like I was nineteen.

"She'll hear us," I said.

"We'll be quiet. Like that time at my parents' house. God, we were awful."

"I'm not awful anymore."

"Sure you are. You just forgot."

She reached for me. I pulled away. And that was the end of it. I left her alone on the deck, and part of me regretted leaving and part of me didn't.

I found Lisa in the bathroom again, this time throwing up for real. I took my place beside her, held her hair while it all came pouring out. Her stomach kept at it for a long time, heaving, emptying itself of the offending matter. Then I helped her clean up. We went to bed. I dreamed about the old days.

* * *

In the morning, Lisa slept late. I woke up and made coffee. I told my friends to go into town for breakfast without me, apologized, explained my wife felt under the weather. They tried to talk me into going, all but Hillary. I promised to meet up with them later.

The house looked like it had been bombed. I started cleaning immediately. I expected to be at it all day again, but after I emptied the ashtrays, threw away the bottles and put the glasses in the dishwasher, I was mostly done. I laid out new towels in the guest bathroom, then wandered around the house looking for more things to put right. That's when Lisa came out of the bedroom. She said she felt better. I was glad to see her but wanted to be alone.

"I'm going for a swim," I said.

Outside on the dock I spotted about a dozen boards that needed to be replaced. I stepped gingerly on the rough planks, wary for splinters. Sunlight blinded me. It came at me from the sky and water. The heat felt good on my shoulders, and I knew the lake would be cold.

When I dove in, I stayed under for a while, eyes open, observing shadowy forms in the depths. I imagined black dirt leaching from my pores, an oily sheen of filth sloughed off by clean water. When my lungs couldn't take the strain, I surfaced. Lisa stood on the dock in her bikini.

"Need some company?" she asked, bronze and glowing, too vivid for this world, seeming to vibrate like a color negative brought to life.

Her cannonball sent billions of droplets soaring skyward, where sunlight transformed them to diamonds. She came up for air and began treading water. She skimmed her hand over the surface to splash me. We laughed and swam in circles, sometimes diving deep, revolving around each other like satellites. She fingered a glistening bikini strap,

129

arched an eyebrow. We stripped, throwing our wet bathing suits on the dock. I swam to her. She kissed me. The water was ice, but her body felt warm.

I remember how we floated on our backs, arms extended, hand in hand—not beside each other but in a straight line, like a hinged pair of paper dolls. A moment. A lifetime. The weight of two lives made buoyant by the thinnest film of surface tension.

"It will always be this way," I said, holding on, suspended between water and light.

MANDY

Stray cat yowls outside the window, giving birth or dying. She sounds like that cunt Mandy. Several hundred miles of fiber optic cable protect Liam as he dumps me. He says, "my friends think you're trying to own me. At first I thought it didn't matter. Guess what—it matters." So I ask, "Who are you fucking? Is it that cunt Mandy?" as an electronic hum replaces his voice. I smash my phone into knives of plastic. Newborn kittens mew beneath the window sill. "Hold me," they say. "Hold me and I'll never leave."

Mule Day

What I'm thinking before the parade is how to get my hands on some of that candy. When you're a kid, you think a lot about candy. I still don't know why grownups go to the parade—maybe for community or history or because they like to see a bunch of horses shitting on Main Street—I don't care. When I was a kid, all I wanted was candy.

Here's how it worked: the nice people in the parade threw candy from the floats, and a bunch of kids would scramble for it and hopefully not get run over by the floats. This one year in particular, I remember a big crowd, which meant lots of kid jockeying for candy. Everybody had lined up on either side of the main drag through town, impatiently waiting for the show to start. And then this clown on a bicycle—an actual, honest-to-god clown on one of those old-fashioned bikes with the one huge wheel in front—rode up and made a slow circle, waving to everybody. He had red hair like Ronald McDonald and a big blue ball on his nose. He reached into his pocket and pulled out a brown paper sack, the kind for taking your lunch to school. The clown grinned real big and tossed the bag in the air. I watched it like a center fielder eyeing a fly ball, and all I could think was how much candy would be inside, maybe the biggest candy-haul in the history of the parade. I glanced at my brother. He looked up at me. We both knew what to do. The two of us and about nine other kids ran at the bag, aiming to catch it like a touchdown pass at the Superbowl. I must have been eleven or twelve years old, just a little older and faster than the rest. I bolted to the head of the pack, never taking my eyes off the bag as it sailed in a delicate arc through the sky. I reached high over all the other kids and snatched it out of the air. It was mine—that sack full of all the candy in the universe. Mine. I opened the bag. And inside was another bag, a clear-plastic Ziploc. But no candy—just this weird sort-of squishy, brown mass. I held up the Ziploc to get a closer look.

"Is it a brownie?" my brother asked. He stood right beside me, tugging my shirt tail.

"Sure," I said. "It's a brownie."

I marched to the nearest garbage can—my face red and burning—to ditch the evidence before anybody saw.

* * *

Miyu listened to my story. She sat across a table from me at Applebee's and sipped a Blue Moon she'd ordered at the bar. She looked at the bottle with a deeply thoughtful expression, then looked up at me again.

"It wasn't a brownie?"

"It was poop, Miyu. The clown threw a bag of poop."

"You tell the weirdest stories," she said.

"And that's what Mule Day means to me. It's not horses or cowboys or rodeos or history. It's this psychopathic clown riding around on a bicycle, his painted-on face locked in a serial-killer grin, and he's just laughing it up and throwing poop."

Just then the waiter came to take our orders. The restaurant was packed, which is rare for an Applebee's, but the parade had drawn people from all over. We'd stood in the foyer for an hour to get a table, and the better part of another to be waited on. The waiter turned out to be a guy from my old high school. I recognized his face immediately but couldn't think of his name. I'd never known him very well. We shook hands, and I acted friendlier than usual to compensate for not remembering his name. He seemed embarrassed to be our waiter. He told me his band was still practicing and getting better all the time. He said he was just waiting tables until the band took off. I

133

wished him good luck. I told him his band was great and everybody from high school believed in them. Then I ordered a hamburger.

"What kind of music do they play?" Miyu asked after he left.

"I didn't know he was in a band," I said.

We waited on our food for a long time. When the hamburgers arrived at last, we dug into them immediately. They were OK. They could have been a lot worse. When you eat at a place like Applebee's, it's best to keep things simple. Miyu ate her entire hamburger, and I wasn't surprised. She was slender and only about five feet tall, but she could eat. Some people think the Japanese eat nothing but fish and rice, but Miyu could put away a hamburger.

"There's a place like this in New York,'" she said, licking the grease off a finger.

"Is it Applebee's?"

"No. Just some hamburger place. Like this but better."

"Applebee's is the worst."

"It's not so bad." Miyu shrugged. "It's cheap, anyway. One meal in the city, just for myself, would cost more than you're paying for both of us. In some ways, you're lucky to have grown up in a place like this." She placed an unnecessary emphasis on *this*, as if Columbia—a perfectly normal Southern town with strip malls and flea markets and a super Walmart—was somehow set apart from the real world, like a quaint seaside village in Scotland, removed from the normal flow of things and left eerily untouched by time.

I made eye contact but was careful not to overdo it. We hadn't slept together since the summer, and I didn't want her to know how much I still thought of her. You have to be careful with girls. You have to be cool. Once a girl knows you love her—when she really knows without any doubt—that's when it's over. That's when she owns you. That's when she gets bored and starts looking around for someone new, someone with that air of mystery you had once but lost. You gave it away. You gave it away because you love her.

"So how do you like it up there?" I said.

"New York is the best," she said. "The greatest. You wouldn't even believe. It's the center of the universe. You should visit. The MOMA. Central Park. There's so much. I can't wait to show you."

"Have you picked a major?"

"You ask all the same questions as my grandmother," she said. "Ask something interesting."

"Why did you want to come here?"

"I missed you," she said, her face lighting up. She reached across the table and took my hand. "I wanted to see you again. I wanted to know where you come from. You used to talk about it so much. I wanted to see for myself."

"How are things with Luther?"

Miyu pulled away. She looked down at her plate. She picked up a French fry and popped it into her mouth. Until now when she'd spoken, she'd looked straight at me with her dark eyes, but when she began again, she stared past me and across the room.

"Luther is good. He's great, actually. He's great. I've never dated someone so—I don't know—intellectual. And he's fun, too. He knows everything about the city, all the best places. I like him. I like him a lot. I love him."

I started to say something but instead lifted my glass to my mouth.

"I guess what you need to know is I'm happy in New York. There's nowhere I'd rather be. And I suppose, even after everything, that you were right—it all worked out for the best. I'm happy. I'm glad I left. I'm happier now than I've been in my life."

When the waiter returned, I asked for the check.

* * *

I drove Miyu around town, past the Family Dollar and Piggly Wiggly and all the push-pull-or-drag used car lots. Traffic thickened as we approached the parade route. The two of us didn't have much to say. My eyes drifted off the road to the tree limbs hanging above. The leaves were only now returning after winter, and the small, green shoots filtered the sun, so it painted abstract patterns on the street below. I pulled into the parking lot at a Fred's discount store. We got out of the car and worked our way through the crowd to get a good view of West 7th Street. Police on motorcycles rode by, sirens blaring. A few minutes later a horse and wagon came up the road, followed by a group of men dressed as frontiersman, then a red convertible with a beauty queen riding in it. The platinum blonde waved to the crowd and smiled her big, fake beauty-queen smile. The parade went on like that for a long time. A lot of guys rode by on horses. They were dressed as cowboys, but they weren't really cowboys. It was all pretend. The fake cowboys looked nice, all clean and fresh, not at all like men who toiled in the fields, in dirt and horse shit. Occasionally one would wave, and everybody in the crowd waved back. Or one would lift up his hat and whoop, and everybody would cheer like he'd done something special. I clapped, too. So did Miyu. All of us were in on it together.

"How long does this last?" Miyu said.

"Hours."

"Did you ever march in the parade in high school, with the band?"

"Every year for four years," I said. "The parade is more fun when you're in it. Avoiding the horse shit requires constant vigilance. It's actually exciting."

Kareem came walking down the sidewalk. Kareem was another guy I knew, a little, from high school. We were never close friends, but we'd talk sometimes. I knew him just well enough that I still recognized him after a few years. He came over when I waved.

"This is bullshit, man," Kareem said.

"That's the point," I said. "Once a year the town comes together to celebrate bullshit."

"It's not just mules they used to sell here, you know," he said. "They sold slaves. Right on the square. Goddamned slave market."

"Oh my god," Miyu said. "I can't even imagine."

"They used to grow cotton here," I said. "Before the Civil War. All the land around here used to be cotton fields."

Kareem pointed to the parade. A guy with a scraggly red beard drove a wagon. He was overweight, with a shiny bald head and denim overalls. He cracked a long whip over his horses. Several rebel flags flew from the wagon.

"You see that shit?" Kareem said.

"Oh my god," Miyu said.

"That's a swastika," Kareem said. "Motherfucking American swastika."

"It's everywhere around here," I said to Miyu. "People fly it from their porches. They put the stickers on their trucks. They think they know what it means but they don't."

"Oh my god," she said.

"You see that horse-driving motherfucker?" Kareem said, pointing.

Miyu nodded.

"Fuck that guy," Kareem said. "His great-granddaddy drove slaves."

Miyu and I walked up the street. The parade kept going and going, and after a while it all looked the same, more horses and mules and fake cowboys and cowgirls. A group walked by, all of them dressed as settlers, the men wearing flannel and the women in gingham dresses. The men were handsome and the women, pretty, and all of them smiled and waved. History classes had taught me that the life of a settler was a hard one of busting sod and living in the dark and isolation. But it was nice to see the reenactors in the parade, all cheerful and lovely. It was better to imagine the settlers that way.

"Jesus," Miyu said. "All of this. It's too much."

"Same thing every year," I said.

"Can we leave?"

"Sure," I said. "I've seen it before."

"I feel hot."

"Come on," I said, motioning to her. "Let's find some shade."

"I feel sick."

"Come on."

"Everything stinks like horse."

Miyu stopped walking. She doubled over, clutching her stomach. She heaved like she would vomit, but nothing came out. I put my hand on her back. Gingerly she stood up again. She looked at the parade. She looked at the crowd. She looked at me, her brown eyes large and watery.

"I hate New York," she said. "I hate Barnard. Everybody's rude. The professors treat us like we're stupid. I hate how, in high school, I was the smartest—being the smartest was who I was, and I liked it— but up there, fuck it. Everybody's a genius. Everybody grew up a child prodigy in some rich fucking family. I hate college. I hate Luther. I hate everything about my life."

I put my arm over her shoulders and pulled her close. I kissed the top of her head. I smelled her hair. The scent was familiar but something I'd forgotten until just then. Out of the corner of my eye I saw a cowboy on horseback. He was young and handsome, like every other cowboy in the parade. He wore a colorful Western shirt, the kind guys buy at American Eagle, the kind that probably didn't even exist back in the olden days.

Miyu wasn't crying but seemed like she might. I kissed her—for real and on the lips—and it felt like decades had passed since that last time. We kept at it awhile, and when we pulled apart she looked just like I remembered from the summer. We smiled and looked away. We watched the parade. The cowboy lifted his hat and whooped and held it high in the air. The crowd cheered. Everybody liked the fake cowboy. A great roar rose up, like thunder from beyond the hills. I didn't know if Miyu would stay with me or disappear to the city again and back to Luther. The cowboy gave another whoop. The sun shone down on his curly hair and the smooth white skin of his face. He looked like an angel from the American West. I kissed Miyu again and felt—suddenly and strangely—that we could travel together back in time and write a new history for ourselves and our world. A better one, kinder and more honest. Our love could right historic wrongs and set the young nation on a truer course. The cowboy kept smiling; the crowd kept cheering. They loved the parade and how it made them feel about themselves and their ancestors and the past. Most of all they loved the handsome cowboy. The history I'd write with Miyu would be more beautiful even than our cowboy angel from the wild frontier of dreams.

You can have it all

You can have every song the Beatles ever recorded. You can have them right now. Just double click on iTunes. Select "Buy now." Boom. Done. It's more than three hundred songs, and you can have every one.

You can have the soundtrack to *Lost in Translation*. You can listen to that song by The Jesus and Mary Chain. And when it's over you can keep listening to the dead air for like 10 minutes until Bill Murray sings "More Than This." You can do it. And you should. Because it's awesome.

Someone blew up a mountain in Appalachia so you could have these things. That's how valuable they are. Think about the mountain sometimes.

You can log on to Facebook and talk to millions of strangers about how the new Weezer album isn't as good as their old stuff, and how they'll spend the next decade churning out album after album without ever recapturing that unexplainable thing they once had.

And when you're done, you can look up all your ex-girlfriends. They're on Facebook. Everybody's on Facebook. The girl you almost fucked after junior prom. And the one you made out with at Megan's party. And you thought the two of you hit it off, only she never returned your calls. According to Facebook she's married. And fat. With kids. And she's really, really into God, and it's after midnight, and you feel lucky she never called you back.

But don't kid yourself. You know why you're online tonight. It's for Her. Her with a capital H. The only one who made you happy. The one with whom you shared a mystical connection. The sarcastic one. The one you never tired of fucking.

You can lurk on her timeline for hours. Scour it for relationship updates. Find out what her friends think about Gwyneth Paltrow on *Glee*. You can check out her pictures. By some dark magic she remains ageless, the same girl who used to share your bed, frozen on the screen for all time.

You can remember the night you spent at the Sheraton. You drank expensive vodka and thought it tasted like regular vodka. You got drunk—so drunk— but still made love on that enormous bed with pillows softer than a litter of newborn kittens.

Or the time in summer session when you meant to study for your French exam, but she insisted on staying up late to watch the Perseids meteor shower, so you spread blankets on the lawn and lay together beneath the clear summer sky. It turned cold after midnight, and you kissed her, and her mouth felt warm. And she wore those tiny shorts, and the moonlight turned her pale legs blue, and you pressed your faces together until she pulled back and pointed straight up, because the stars were falling, falling, burning white trails across the universe.

You can linger a moment longer among her pictures. You can find the one you snapped at the beach. Her wet skin glistening. Red bikini skin-tight. Her lips, parted slightly, almost blue from the ocean, so blue they just kill you.

You can unbutton your pants. You can slip your hands beneath the elastic of your boxers. You can jack off to her memory one last time. Just one last time.

And you can lie in bed in a room dark but for the faint illumination from your iPod. You can muse about how *In Rainbows* was a perfectly lovely idea but all you want from Radiohead is more "Creep." You can ask yourself how those old Jewel songs infiltrated your playlist. You can listen and remember. And after the songs end you can see the battery is mostly drained of the electricity supplied by a coal-fired power plant. You know this. This is a problem. It is making the planet retarded. The weather and harvests are fucked.

Some nice brown family did not eat tonight because you listen to songs and look at pictures. You can't stop. You'll download something tomorrow. Something by Iggy Pop. You'll look at her picture and fuck the consequences.

Because it's worth it.

Maybe it's worth it.

Please.

Tell me it's worth it.

Jamie

Jamie liked to say he was a man's man. He liked even more for other people to say it. Jamie liked shooting guns and shooting up. He paid too much for a motorcycle and drove it everywhere until the crash. Jamie never wore a helmet. Jamie laughed at helmets.

It was because he'd totaled the bike that I had to pick him up for the party. The party was for Jamie. In the morning, he would leave for basic training. This was back when there was a war in Iraq, and Jamie wanted to fight. Jamie liked to say he was born for war.

When I showed up at his place, he was smoking on the front steps beside an enormous canvas duffle bag. He hefted it into my trunk and then squeezed himself into my passenger seat. Jamie was almost too big for my car. Heavily muscled. His body had a rugged seriousness about it. Thick hair on his chest and forearms. Tattoos of dice and naked women. He was not the sort of man the engineers had in mind while designing my fuel-efficient hybrid. Jamie belonged in monster trucks and up-armored Humvees.

"So, I guess we should talk about it," I said, pulling onto the highway.

"Talk is cheap." Jamie flashed me his who-gives-a-fuck smile. "Drive faster. I need a beer."

He looked out the window and told me Allison would be at the party.

"I won't miss much about this town," he said. "But I'll miss fucking Allison."

He said the words with no discernible emotion, as if reading from a script.

Jamie had been my friend for about as long as I can remember, and for most of those years he'd been my best friend. I met him in third grade. I think we'd always gone to school together, even back to kindergarten, but at first he was just another classmate, a face I recognized but didn't connect with. Then one day some douchebag—his name was Darren or Duane or something douchey like that—started calling me names in front of all the girls at recess. I wore this Mickey Mouse shirt, and Duane laughed and said it looked faggy—which I suppose it did, but anyway, I was like nine years old, and he was a dick to bring it up.

I shrugged it off and walked away, but Duane wasn't finished. He followed me around the playground laughing and calling me a fag. I didn't even know what the word meant but understood by the way he said it that it wasn't nice. Duane might have kept it up indefinitely if Jamie hadn't gotten in his face and told him to shut his ignorant mouth. Duane responded the way any third-grader would, by daring Jamie to make him. Jamie smiled at this.

When the punch came, it was like lightning. Through the fog of memory, I recall a flash of light, a sonic boom, an angelic choir holding a single note. I watched Jamie's fist connect with Duane's face and felt I had witnessed something extraordinary, like the Incredible Hulk hurling the Red Skull into the sun or God carrying light into a universe of darkness.

Duane fell down, clutching his nose and crying. Jamie grabbed my arm and told me to run before the teachers showed up. Later I caught my breath by the swings. Jamie asked if I was OK, and I cried a little, but Jamie didn't make me feel too embarrassed. He asked if I wanted to play on the swings, so that's what we did for the rest of recess, and at some indefinable point while swinging we became friends. I remember Jamie impressed me by swinging real high. He wore a new pair of L.A. Gears—also impressive.

"Someday I'll be an astronaut," he said. "Someday I'll fly out into space."

I believed him. I imagined him piloting a rocket to distant stars, discovering hidden planets and strange new life forms. I imagined him firing a photon pistol, righting wrongs with his bravery and martial skill, he alone keeping the galaxy at peace. At that moment, watching him pull against the chains and point his toes at the sky, I believed Jamie could do anything.

* * *

As I drove him to his going-away party he talked about football, even though he knew I didn't care about football.

"Manning got blitzed after the snap," he said. "Manning got crushed."

I was dimly aware of who Manning might be. Jamie went on, telling me who else got crushed. I looked at Jamie's stubble and wondered what our lives would be like without so much history behind us. I mean if we were only now meeting for the first time. Would we even like each other? Or would he think I was a joke? I worried that our true friendship had burnt out years ago. Not that it mattered. Jamie would catch a bus in the morning. Jamie would cross an ocean and fight a war and maybe come home in a box.

I pulled into the campground and parked in a gravel lot. We walked along a trail for about five minutes to get to the tents. The sun was setting and neither of us felt like talking. It was just me and Jamie with no bullshit between us, like old times, and summer was ending, and the air felt crisp like falling leaves.

When we got to the tents everybody crowded around Jamie, everybody wanted to talk to him and shake his hand one last time. I let them have him. I sat on a log by the fire and pulled a beer out of a Styrofoam cooler. I drank slow. I don't tell this to many people, but I hate beer. The party was mostly full of Jamie's friends, guys he'd met

145

on construction crews and at bars. I guess I knew everybody at the party, but we weren't close. They were just faces to me.

Allison hovered. She tried her best to always stand by Jamie's side, to rest a hand on his bicep or put her arm around him. Jamie had dumped her more than a year prior, or tried to. She never stopped hanging around, and—mostly out of inertia—Jamie never stopped fucking her.

Dave tried to feed the fire with some torn pages of newspaper. Jamie told him he was doing it wrong. He grabbed a plastic bottle of lighter fluid and squeezed a stream into the flames. A fireball erupted, making a noise like "fwomp." Nobody died. Allison laughed and laughed. I noticed she wore her black tank top. Jamie had told her once he liked it.

We sat around and drank and eventually overcooked some burgers. Roger told us how *Die Hard* was the best movie ever. Jamie called bullshit. He said it had nothing on *The Rock*.

"You remember that part where the big guy pulls a knife on Nicholas Cage and goes, 'I'll take pleasure in gutting you, boy'?" Jamie said. "That's some funny shit."

Jamie repeated the line all night, punctuating his stories about sports and hunting. The night was full of talk, talk about anything but the army or war.

Eventually Allison yawned.

"I'm turning in," she said, giving Jamie a long and serious look, letting her hand linger on his arm before strutting off to their tent. Pretty soon, most everybody went to sleep, leaving me and Jamie to stare into what was left of the fire.

"Sounds like Allison wants company," I said.

"She'll wait," he said. "She always does."

He rummaged through the cooler for another beer.

"I'm just the right amount drunk," he said. "I want to keep it going, you know? I don't want it to stop."

He cracked a can and stood up, looked at the trail leading into the woods.

"Let's go to the lake. I need some air. Need to move my legs."

"I don't know," I said. "It's late."

"Come on. I need to see some trees before they ship me to the desert. Come on. Do this for me. Just this one thing."

I shrugged and followed him into the woods. It was dark under the trees but light enough to make out the trail as it wound down the hill to the docks. The woods smelled thick and damp. An owl hooted somewhere above us.

"I won't lie," Jamie said, scratching his scalp. "The woods at night freak me the fuck out."

Soon the trees opened to show off the sky and lake. Jamie walked to the end of the dock and sat with his legs swinging over the ledge. I sat beside him. A breeze blew off the water.

"Do you worry much about the war?" I said.

"Sure," he said. "I don't know. I don't want to think about it. It's not real yet, you know? It's just some shit that hasn't happened. Talking about it will only make it real."

Jamie burped and crumpled his empty can. He tossed it into the lake, where it splashed and made ripples that came back to us. He leaned toward me, placed one hand gently on my arm. I felt the stubble of his jaw in the space between my head and shoulder, his lips gently pressing against my neck.

"Don't start that again," I said.

I pulled away, stood up and paced around the dock like a mother hen, arms crossed, face drawn into a frown.

"That can't happen," I said. "I'm not ... that can't happen."

Jamie said nothing. He stared out into the lake. I sat beside him after a while, asked if everything was OK. He sobbed. He told me not to leave. I promised I wouldn't. For a long time I listened to his breathing, watched his shoulders rise and fall. Jamie always breathed like he was trying to vacuum up all the air on the planet, but that night it was different, softer, like he was some small animal from a wildlife documentary, like he was the last of his kind, and he knew it, like he would never be anything but alone.

I remember waking up with a sore back from sleeping on the dock. The sun burned white and stung my eyes.

"Shit," Jamie said, rubbing his face. "What time is it?"

When we got back to the tents, Dave had cooked eggs. Jamie told everybody we stole a canoe, then lost the paddles on the lake. Allison sat away from the rest of us. She ate in silence and stared at her plate.

The party broke up around eleven. I drove Jamie to the bus station. I felt like I hadn't showered in a week. Jamie stared out the window. I wished he would say something, even if it was only some lame story about football.

"I guess we should talk about it," I said.

"Ain't nothing to talk about," he said, watching the cars on the highway. He pointed at a black Chevy Silverado.

"Look at that one," he said. "That's the real shit. That's some cowboy shit."

We talked about cars all the way to the bus station. I remember how he stood with his duffle bag at his feet, watching the other passengers board the bus.

"The Army," he said. "Why did I join the goddamn Army?"

He scratched his jaw.

"I used to want to be an astronaut."

"I know," I said. "I remember."

He turned to me and smiled.

"I know you know."

He stood beside me for a moment longer before boarding. When the door closed, it looked like an airlock sealing off a space capsule.

That's the last time I saw Jamie.

Sometimes, I like to imagine there's a planet out in space inhabited by a race of roughnecks and cowboys. Where they rope steer all day and climb mountains, huddle around campfires at night drinking beer from cans and telling big stories. Where they hunt for their food, and they fashion crude clothing from the hides of their kills. Where their muscles have grown hard and ropey, and their skin is brown leather from a lifetime under the sun. Sometimes I like to imagine Jamie is the first astronaut to discover this planet. Like he flew there in a rocket. Like he never looked back. Like he landed, and he stepped out of the capsule and saw that everybody had gathered in anticipation.

To greet him.

To welcome him home.

About the Author

Alex Miller is a writer and graphic designer. He is the author of the novella "Osama bin Laden is Dead." His stories have appeared in *Fifth Wednesday Journal, Maudlin House* and *WhiskeyPaper,* among other journals. He lives in Pittsburgh, Pennsylvania.

About the Press

Unsolicited Press is a small press based in Portland, Oregon. The press, founded in 2012, publishes literary fiction, nonfiction, and poetry by emerging and award-winning authors.

Learn more at www.unsolicitedpress.com.